ALL AROUND THE YEAR

ALL AROUND THE YEAR

Liz Shakespeare

LETTERBOX BOOKS

First published 2013
by
Letterbox Books
Littleham
Bideford
Devon
EX39 5HW

www.lizshakespeare.co.uk

ISBN 978-0-9516879-3-2

MIX
Paper from
responsible sources
FSC
www.fsc.org
FSC® C014540

Printed and bound by SRP Ltd, Exeter

ACKNOWLEDGEMENTS

I am very grateful to Shirley Cowling, Alison Harding and Nora Bendle for their support and encouragement over the years; to Kate Cryan for taking the time to read the manuscript and for her advice and reassurance; and to my son Ben for his hard work and endless patience when designing the cover.

CONTENTS

New Beginnings

Penelope hesitated before slowly opening the shed door. The two mountain bikes leant side by side against the work bench, their handlebars and pedals entwined. Gently, she moved Dan's bike away and wiped the worst of the dust from her own with a rag, then backed it out of the garden shed. As she closed the door, she looked away so she would not have to see Dan's bike standing alone. She stood still for a few moments, staring at the sparse, frozen grass and empty flower beds in the small back garden and the frost still remaining on the roof of the house. She could put the bike away again and go back indoors. But it was weeks since she had been out for a walk or a cycle and she had hoped the fresh air and exercise might distract her, just a little. She twisted her long fair hair up out of the way and fastened her helmet, then pushed her bike out into the back lane and cycled on to the main road.

Barnstaple's streets were almost deserted, the raw cold and post-Christmas frugality keeping people at home by their fires; there were few pedestrians and only occasional cars heading in the direction of the out-of-town superstores for their Sunday shopping. Penelope turned into Bear Street and passed the shuttered second-hand shops, the takeaways and the tattooist. An overlooked Christmas tree was strung above one shop front. Christmas. Was it soon? But no, of course not, it was over. She had forgotten, because it had been unlike any other Christmas she had known.

She cycled past the allotments, then stood on the pedals and sped past the cemetery with its roadside sentinels of leafless trees, then past the rows of identical houses on the estate until she had left the town behind. There were empty fields between the houses and the sky was cold and grey.

She and Dan had surfed whenever they could but when the surf was flat they occasionally went cycling. They had come this way a few times but more often they went towards Exmoor, sometimes putting the bikes on the back of the car when they wanted to cycle off-road all day. He nearly always rode in front so her view of the Devon countryside had always contained his form, his lean determined back and tanned legs powering ahead, his dark hair curling below his helmet. Every now and then he would glance back to see that she was still with him and she would catch his smile as he turned. Now the road stretched emptily before her. She pushed on up the hill, past stark trees and colourless hedges until the valley narrowed and deepened and she turned off at Collard Bridge and crossed the track bed of the long-disused railway.

She stopped on the old packhorse bridge, leant on the parapet and looked down at the grey-brown water of the River Yeo creeping relentlessly beneath the tangle of lifeless branches. She pulled off her glove and reached out to the ivy leaves which clung to the cold stone parapet, the only green things she could see, plucked a leaf and held it for a moment. It was limp and waxy in her hand and she dropped it into the river and watched while it passed slowly beneath the bridge and disappeared from sight.

'Dan is dead.' She said it again. 'Dan is dead.' How ever often she said it, the words seemed meaningless.

The previous evening her mother had phoned from Uganda again. Penelope had turned off the television and curled up on the sofa, breathing deeply to control the sobs which were released by the sound of her mother's voice.

'No, I'm all right Mum, honest.'

She was aware that her mother's pain was, if anything, greater than her own because whereas she felt numb and unbelieving for much of the time, her mother suffered constantly on her behalf and wanted to take the pain away from her. When the pain came, it was unbearable; nothing helped; no one could take it away. Her mother worried about her being alone, although Penelope assured her she could be with friends if she wanted. She told her mother how she had had dinner with friends on Friday, the first time she had tried to socialise. They had been gentle with her, talking carefully about things that would not upset her, remembering to mention Dan's name so that she would know they had not forgotten him. She had stayed the night alone in the unfamiliar bed and despite the comfort of waking to the sound of movement and voices in the house, had insisted on leaving after breakfast.

'Sweetheart, you know I could be there with you in a couple of days if you needed me, you only have to ask and I'll be on my way. Promise you'll tell me if you need me. I hate to think of you there on your own.'

Her mother paused and Penelope heard her father's voice prompting in the background.

'Now I must tell you, we've been looking at houses today on the internet. We've seen one in Georgeham, a lovely thatched cottage that's just come on the market. I know you can't make up your mind yet but if you do decide to stay in Devon, you know we would still love to come down to be near you.'

Her parents were due to retire in a few months. Two years ago they had both given up their teaching jobs in Surrey and had gone to Uganda as volunteers to run a primary school. When their contracts came to an end, the plan had been sell their house in Guildford and move to Devon to be near Penelope and Dan.

'I know, Mum, thanks. Nothing feels right at the moment. I hate the thought of leaving here but I don't know if I can stay without him. We had so many plans…'

She felt her voice began to waver again and her mother was quiet for a few moments, before struggling to speak again.

'It will get easier darling, it will take a long time but you *will* be happy again, one day. It's all so new now. When are you due to see the doctor again?'

Her doctor had offered something to help her sleep in the days after Dan's death but she had not taken it. He had given her a certificate and was cautious about her determination to return to work two weeks ago, insisting that she must see him again.

'On Wednesday, after my shift. I'll be ok. I'll tell him how I'm feeling. I'll ring you afterwards.'

'The spring will be here soon, darling; that makes everything a bit easier. January is always a difficult month.'

'It's so cold now!'

'And it's so hot here, 35 degrees for the last few days! Even at night it seems no cooler. I'm sitting here in a vest and shorts and the perspiration is running off me. The children in school don't seem to notice it but we find it very difficult to match their enthusiasm when we're so hot. We've had rain too and you can almost see the crops growing.'

Leaning on the cold stone bridge looking at the bare trees and frozen grass, it was hard to believe that there was anywhere in the world that was warm and vibrant.

Her mother had rung off and Penelope had wrapped the throw that covered the sofa around her and sat hugging her knees for a long time. Everything in the room reminded her of Dan. The sofa they bought from the second-hand shop in Bear Street. The bookcase, holding the travel books and nursing manuals, that Dan made from an old packing case. On the wall - that they painted together when they first moved in - the framed photo of the two of them surfing together. There was the memory of their first visit to the house, Dan catching her eye as they were shown around and both of them knowing that this house would be the one, then the excitement as they planned the changes they would make. The memories that were held in the house were like a film playing before her eyes, Dan smiling, talking, laughing, always enthusiastic, always so alive. They did not console her but only served to emphasise his absence. Keeping the throw around her, she went out through the kitchen and opened the back door. The air was still and bitingly cold and the light from the kitchen shone out on to the frosted grass and illuminated the bare stems of the shrub they had planted alongside the fence. She stepped out on to the patio and looked up at the star-filled sky.

They had stood here together one night after Dan had downloaded Google Sky map on to his phone; he held it up and together they pointed out the constellations and the planets and she leaned up against him to share his warmth.

'There, look, the North Star!' he had said, 'Amazing to think that for hundreds of years it has helped people find their way.'

Tonight the stars glittered coldly and, try as she might, she could not identify any of them.

To stay in Devon without Dan would be to feel his absence every moment of every day and night. It was too soon to know what she should do but she would have to make a decision before April when her parents retired. If she returned to London, she was afraid it would feel as if she had never known him, as if it had all been a dream.

They had met the summer before last at Croyde. She had seen him on the beach with some tourist surfers, and as she walked back in the warm afternoon sun there he was again, hanging his wetsuit outside the chalet where he was staying with a group of friends. They said 'Hi', then glimpsed each other that evening in the Thatch. Gradually, they both moved to talk with friends on the periphery of the groups they were with, until they were close enough to greet each other. They discovered that they lived just a few miles apart in London and they talked about the places they had travelled to; she had been to Indonesia and Australia, he to Thailand, Vietnam and Laos, but not on a surfing trip. She was the better surfer because she had been coming to Croyde since she was a child. He hadn't minded when she showed him some moves the next day and that evening they left their friends and went to the beach, to lie on the soft, forgiving sand and talk and share some beers. The sand dunes rising behind them hid them from the village and throughout the night they faced the roar of the invisible surf, until the sun came up. She had known, then, that they would be together. Croyde had always been a special place for her; the bay of tawny sand encircled by gentle green hills, the thatched cottages and pubs and music, and the constant soothing roar of the waves which, her mother said, drew people to the sea because it resembled the sounds heard in the womb. Now Croyde became *their* village. It was the surfing that first brought them together and then anything seemed possible. They could live here and surf every weekend and life would be one long holiday.

It was easy. She got the job she wanted at the hospital and Dan was able to work from home. They found a house they could afford in Barnstaple and by spring they had moved in and it seemed as if her life - her happy childhood, the years of studying and then travelling - had always been moving towards this; the warmth and love in their home together and the weekends of surfing with friends at Croyde. They talked, with wonder, of a future with children.

Sometimes they surfed when she had finished her shift. She told Dan about her day while they drove alongside the estuary and through Braunton's congested streets, then along the narrow road that hugged the coast, winding between the steep gorse-covered hills and the sheer drop to the bright azure sea. When Croyde came into view and they saw the lines of surf running endlessly and unimpeded into the horseshoe-shaped bay, they would assess the swell and as they swung into the car park they would point out the familiar vehicles. There was still warmth in the evening sun as it streamed across the glittering, expansive ocean into her eyes, blinding her as she paddled out beyond the surf with Dan, and she knew that after the waiting and the watching, after the moment came and they shared in the exhilaration as the sea carried them, braced and balancing towards the shore, they would sit together on the sand as the sinking sun performed its evening magic, transforming the bay with its flush of colour.

Then Dan had been killed. He was usually so careful. He was in a hurry; he hadn't expected ice on the roads in early November. If only she had rung him from work she could have told him about the ice, she could have warned him to be careful on his motorbike. But she hadn't even known that he was going to go out. Her mother had said it over and over again, 'It's not your fault. It was an accident.'

She turned her back to the river and leaned on the bridge. She had returned to work two weeks ago. Those early weeks were a blur now. The initial shock which made her body shake uncontrollably, then the crying that would not stop, and her mother who held her, hour after hour. Christmas at her brother's house. Then after New Year she had insisted that she would go back to their home and her job and had made her mother leave after a few days. She had hoped that being at work and being busy might make it more bearable, at least some of the time. Returning to the hospital the first time and having to walk past A&E to reach her ward had been the hardest part. She was determined to keep going, to ride the waves of grief and not let herself be swept under. It was what Dan would have wanted.

She had always felt that she was good at her job but recently it had been different, as if she was seeing her patients as individuals for the first time. It was as if a layer of her skin had been removed making her sensitive to everything and everyone she touched. An elderly lady had been brought in this week, conscious and able to answer simple questions but bemused, as if she didn't understand how she came to be there. Penelope checked her records and took her blood pressure, then explained gently that she would be staying in hospital for a while because she had had a stroke, and she just stared back, troubled but uncomprehending. Penelope had seen dozens of similar cases but this time she felt a shock of recognition and had taken the woman's hand, for the first time understanding how it might feel.

'It will get easier; we'll look after you.' She realised she was echoing her mother's words.

She and Dan had leant on this bridge together the last time they had come here. It was autumn, a tranquil day without a breath of wind and the leaves were falling, russet and copper and yellow, floating from the interwoven branches, coming to rest on the ground or landing on the river to sail gently under the bridge. Now the leaves were rotten, frozen in mounds. What had they talked of? Hadn't there been a disagreement, a mild falling-out? Dan could be as obstinate as she could herself but he was quicker to forgive, his annoyance turning to a smile and a caress in a moment. She remembered the warmth of his arms around her, his chest pressing against her, the sound of his breath close to her ear. She pulled the zip of her fleece further up and put her foot back on the pedal. It was too cold to stand around.

The track climbed steeply and she had to dismount before the top. She was unfit; she had had no exercise since Dan had died and she seemed to be tired all the time. She never used to find work so tiring.

The frozen track ran along the contour of the hill below a dense, silent conifer wood which swallowed up the weak January daylight and cast a deep shadow. Below the track, coppiced woodland sloped to the valley floor where there was a muddle of old corrugated sheds, an abandoned JCB and discarded tyres under fallen branches. She pushed on. She skidded a little on the frozen mud which had been churned up by horses and scrambler bikes on warmer days. If Dan had been in front, mud spattered up his back from his tyres, he would have turned to warn her when it was slippery.

'Watch out on this bit!'

As she rode, she lifted one hand, then the other, to her mouth and blew through her gloves to warm her cold fingers.

The track branched and she stopped, bringing silence as the whirr of her tyres ceased. Beyond and above her the Chelfham viaduct stretched across the valley like a giant frozen in mid-stride, a huge incontrovertible fact cutting across the soft contours. It appeared incongruous now, dwarfing the buildings at its feet, but Dan had read up about it and told her about the steam trains they would have seen if they had stood on this spot a hundred and fifty years ago. The trains and the track were long gone and only a shallow depression through the valley showed where they had run. There were plans to reinstate the line, Dan had said. Now there was no movement, and no sound except the rasping of her breath. She and Dan had taken the steep track which led up the hill, so steep that they had climbed in the lowest gear until they had reached the top out of breath and with aching legs and had thrown themselves on to the grass to lie together and gaze at the view before them, the folded valley and glowing hills. She stared again at the viaduct towering above her. Its immobility and its silence were frightening. She turned away and cycled to the road. She would take the lower route today.

On the day of her doctor's appointment she went home to change into her jeans then opened the back door to fetch her bike. There had been some light rain in the night and it was still cold, but a little weak sunlight caught the bare silvery twigs of the shrub which grew against the old wooden fence. She picked up a watering can which had lain forgotten on its side in the flower bed, and a crisp-packet blown in from the garden next door. Underneath, pushing through the still partially frozen earth, was a small green nub like the nose or fingertip of a small creature struggling to escape from the frozen ground. She reached down to touch it, at first thinking it to be a piece of plastic on the surface of the bed, and saw that it had two parts pushing from a papery sheath. She rubbed it gently in her fingers and saw that there was another closer to the fence and another to her right. Daffodils. When she and Dan moved into the house, they had been flowering all along this side of the garden, cream and golden yellow with orange centres. They had been there all the time under the ground, little kernels of energy stored in warmer times and waiting, even in the weeks after he died, and then pushing upwards through the cold earth when she thought everything was dead. She sat back on her heels and stared at them.

She walked to the shed then paused, placing her hand tentatively on her abdomen, trying to identify a sensation that might be the stirring of the imagination but seemed familiar, like the memory of something previously overlooked.

'Dan...' It was the first time she had been able to speak to him, the first time she had felt that he was there, with her and a part of her. 'Dan, I think I may... I'm going to see the doctor, Dan.'

As she leaned against the shed door, it seemed that the garden was full of daffodils again, the hedge was greening and flowers opening, and she understood that the spring would come again, year after year after year.

Valentine's Day

Graham smiled at Debbie sitting opposite him and then gazed past her and around the pub again. The owners had done it up a treat, traditional, olde worlde, just as a pub should be. The red velvet curtains were new, Debbie said, and the seat covers. It was a good choice, coming here. The owners had made an effort, what with the candles and the red rose on each table and the impressive menu, and they obviously had a successful business but of course they'd moved from away and had bought the pub outright and that made quite a difference. It was a struggle for those that had to pay rent.

'It was a good choice, wasn't it, coming here?'

She smiled, so he supposed she agreed.

He and Debbie looked good together sitting there in the candlelight, Debbie in her black dress and he'd put on a tie and his best trousers. A neat-looking couple, that's what people used to say of them because neither of them had put on weight although they were in their early fifties. 'You see, it's good for you,' he used to say to customers, 'fruit and veg, five a day. Look at us! It's easy when you own a greengrocer's!'

They'd never missed a Valentine's Night. He was traditional like that; he liked to do things right but it had been hard to achieve in recent years what with the shop and other things. He used to say to her, 'We may be losing everything else but we mustn't lose that.' Twenty-nine years they had been married. He never thought that things would turn out like this, at the start.

John and Sandy Glover were over there sitting by the window. Debbie turned around every now and then to look at them. John was wearing a tight white shirt with half the buttons undone and was leaning back in his chair. Debbie had suggested they join up for coffee after the meal but he wasn't too fussed because John would only tell them about the

11

building trade, how busy he was. He was working up the hill where the estate was being extended, his roofers already on the first house while a bulldozer cut into the old pasture to level more sites for him. Graham and Debbie had driven up one day to look but had not liked to get out of the car in case someone thought they were interested in buying. John was building a new house for himself and Sandy and the kids, a big place with a bathroom for every bedroom. He would know that Graham and Debbie were renting now.

Debbie was watching the young couple sitting in the corner. The chap had low-slung jeans and gelled hair and had moved his chair around so that he was beside his girlfriend; he had his hand on her thigh and was kissing her neck. They were both laughing and she was trying to push him away.

Graham thought it best not to look.

'I wonder when we'll get our starters. John and Sandy haven't got theirs yet either.'

Debbie turned around and waved to them.

'Your hair looks nice. It suits you like that.'

He always tried to notice. He did make an effort.

Last Valentine's Day they had just given up the shop and he'd been let out of hospital the previous week. It was a struggle, to tell the truth. But he said to her,

'We've still got each other, haven't we? We've never missed yet and we mustn't this year.' And they didn't.

More shops had closed since they had given up - there had been two more just since Christmas. He'd forgotten to tell Debbie the latest news.

'Walters's went overnight, so I was told today. Rent unpaid of course and all the stock gone with them.'

Another family business, second generation. No one seemed to know where they had gone even though they'd lived in the town all their lives. Not even her elderly mother knew, so people said.

At least he and Debbie didn't do that. At least they did everything properly and didn't owe anything, not as far as the business was concerned anyway. He was thankful for that.

But his granddad - he would have had something to say about it.

Here were the starters. He was having the soup. What was it called?

'Pass me the menu again so I can see what the soup is, Debs.'

You had to be careful not to set the menu alight on that candle. Spicy Tomato and Red Pepper Soup. And Debbie's was the Cocktail of Prawns and Hot-Smoked Salmon.

It was his great-grandfather that had started the business. He was the first one in the town to have bananas, so they said. The farmers used to look at them and say, 'What d'you call 'em then, boy, banes?' They thought they were beans! Folk came from all over town to look at the bananas and he couldn't get anyone to buy them because they had never seen such a thing before. He had to tell people how to eat them.

'Do you remember that story about great-granddad and the bananas, Debbie?'

He'd told that tale a time or two. He used to tell it in the shop when customers were buying bananas. Then there was the story about him helping his granddad when he was only four or five, carrying cauliflowers and cabbage out from their storage in a dark and dusty passage and a customer said, 'You'd think he was on Crackerjack, carrying all those caulis!' He'd never forgotten that. 'You'd think he was on Crackerjack!' Just a little tacker, he'd been.

All gone now. That dark, dusty passage was a hallway for the two new flats now, all light and clean and modern. But all the memories, where were they?

'Good soup, this. Are your prawns all right?'

In the old days it was all local produce; it wasn't called that because people just took it for granted that it was local, but now it was thought to be something special. In the old days they'd have cabbages and leeks and root veg and local apples and that was about all in the winter, so his granddad used to say. Later on, there were always tomatoes and salad brought in from foreign parts, and oranges and bananas all the year round until in the end you could get anything anytime you wanted and you put a special ticket on things that were 'local produce'.

It was his own business, his and Debbie's, passed down through the generations and it was his life. Opening up early on a spring morning he'd look up to see the sun slanting into the High Street and reflecting from the windows of the fine old buildings which were three and four storeys high and every one different from its neighbour, and he'd look at the shop windows below – the card shop, the shoe shop, the delicatessen – and admire how well they were arranged, though none so good as his. He'd put out the red Braeburns, green Granny Smiths and the mottled Coxes, sometimes giving them a polish to make them gleam, the tomatoes arranged in their paper wrappers with their stalks on top, a pyramid of cauliflowers, and the mushrooms so fresh and white they hardly looked real. He'd be in and out with the trays while Debbie set up inside and he'd be calling 'good morning' to the shop assistants and office workers walking in to work because he'd known them all. When he'd finished he would stand back and admire the display, straighten out the green cloth and give the window a quick polish.

He liked to talk to the customers. He was good at that.

'Lovely strawberries today, Mrs West.'

'The watercress is fresh in today, if you want some for your tea. Now, will there be anything else for you?'

He knew to ask Mrs Beer about her husband's heart, to tell Miss Cole he'd got some nice green bananas out the back. That's what people used to like, the personal touch.

It was different later, when the new supermarket opened and trade dropped away so much it was hard to keep things fresh. You couldn't afford to keep throwing stock away but who wants to buy grey, wrinkled mushrooms? The shop looking shabby and no money to repaint it. Standing in the doorway and looking up the almost deserted street, not knowing whether to call out a greeting when someone hurried past with their face averted. Then the time when it all got too much and he stood there shouting, shouting those things for everyone to hear. Shouting until Debbie called the doctor, and the doctor came and took him away.

Another couple had come into the pub, in their thirties probably. They went up to the bar and the landlord pointed out a table. The woman had a very tight skirt and red lipstick. Outsiders. It was nearly all outsiders, these days. At least they wouldn't know about him.

He still couldn't bear to walk past the shop, not if he could help it. A candle shop now, that's what it was. Candles! What use were candles to anyone? Hadn't they all got electricity now? But it managed to stay open, the candle shop. How could it manage to stay open when he couldn't? When he had the shop, naturally he supported the other businesses in the High Street but he didn't like to go there now. There were still some people there who knew him and he certainly wasn't going to go to that other greengrocer. Several of the shops were boarded up anyway; there weren't many left, not those that sold things you needed. Unless you wanted candles. Or a cup of coffee. They could drink coffee at home, him and Debbie, they didn't need to sit with other people and drink coffee.

Debbie did the shopping in Lidl now, like everyone else. Well, working there, she got a discount of course. She had started off on fifteen hours a week and they put her with the fruit and veg on account of her experience. He couldn't have done it, working there and watching their old customers doing their shopping, the ones who had put them out of business by going to the supermarket all the time. She didn't seem to mind, she said she enjoyed the company. But now she was down to seven hours and was stacking shelves. She didn't talk about it very much.

'Very nice soup, that was.'

John and Sandy had finished their starters too. That young couple had hardly started theirs, by the look of it. He and Debbie had never been like that, not demonstrative, certainly not in public.

If they'd had children. Perhaps he could have made the business work, if they'd had children, and if the children had wanted to go into the business. Continue it on, fifth generation. But the town centre was dead; he could never have kept it going, even if they'd had children.

She still felt it, he knew that. Any woman would. They both did.

She was still a pretty woman. Look at her; miles away she was, daydreaming.

'Be careful, the plates are hot.' The waitress was very young and had a high, sing-song voice.

What was his? Grilled Sirloin Steak with a Smooth Stout and Stilton Sauce. And Debbie had Sliced Duck Breast with Morello Cherries.

'Looks nice, doesn't it?'

She nodded. Was she happy? She didn't say.

When he started the new job it was a relief to be doing something again after all the hard times and then the shame of losing everything. After the months at home. Funny, he hadn't thought of the shop as a job, it was just what they did, he and Debbie, what his father had done and his father before him. Now, in his job, he didn't get to handle the fruit and veg anymore, just lift crates; that was all.

He'd drive to the depot, load up the fruit and veg, and he'd look at his list and think – where do I have to go today then? He'd drive up and down the A386 with the county laid out before him, fields and woods stretching for miles like a patchwork bedspread pulled over an unmade bed and hardly a house to be seen, Dartmoor rising like a threat beyond it all and then the sky and the gathering clouds. Huge skies. He'd never realised before how big the skies were, being on the High Street all day with high buildings all around. He saw signposts to places he'd hardly heard of. Broadwoodwidger. Honeychurch. He'd never seen so much of Devon and it was an eye-opener to tell the truth because everything was so changed. He'd drive through a village looking for the place where he was to make his delivery and all the verges would be mown, the houses would be renovated and have new windows and fresh paintwork, the gates freshly varnished and new cars on the paved driveways. There would be lawns and terraces with big umbrellas to keep the sun off, stables with horses looking over the doors. He got to see how the other half live. But where were all the other people, all the ordinary everyday folk who used to live in the country when the roads were muddy and the cottages rundown? All those years in the shop looking out across the High Street to the ironmongers and to Woolworths, he hadn't realised how things had changed. The people who used to be his customers weren't the ones who lived now in the neat villages with the big lawns.

It felt like work, driving for miles and delivering to hotels and restaurants and pubs. Shops as well, not that there were many left. He didn't like going in the shops because some of the people knew who he was. They didn't say anything but they knew. *He's* the one who used to run the greengrocer's in the High Street; *he's* the one we heard about, that's what they thought.

He missed handling the produce. Just pick up a box, put it on the van. Drive the van. Stop the van, take out the box. He'd look at it as he carried it in; good quality caulis, he'd think, nice fresh spinach, but it isn't mine, not any more, I'm just the delivery man. And he missed the people, the personal touch. The people in the hotels and restaurants, they were not interested in *him*.

Sometimes he would deliver to places that he and Debbie used to visit on Sundays years ago, in the early days when they used to get out more. Gidleigh. Lydford. When they went to Lydford they used to have a wander around the castle then sit on the grassy slope for a while to watch children rolling down the hill, over and over, until they were distant shapes at the bottom of the hill. He and Debbie watched the children rolling and talked about the business and the customers and whatever gossip was going round the town; the stock they needed to buy in that week, more of this, less of that. They never ran out of things to say, then, in the early days. They were happy, just the two of them, in the beginning. They'd have some tea in that nice tea shop and afterwards they'd have a walk. They didn't go down in the Gorge because it was too steep and dark. They used to walk along to the edge of the moor and look up at it, its bleak barrenness rising above them. Then turn and walk back through the trees. Hold hands. Admire the houses and say perhaps they could move there one day. If the business did well. They'd say it would be a good place to bring up children.

He thought of that when he went there now.

The waitress was slow to clear the plates away. Perhaps she had forgotten them.

'Has the waitress forgotten us, do you think?'

John and Sandy were on the pudding already. They were on their second bottle of wine so they must have booked a taxi. Well, they could afford it; his business was doing well.

'Shall we have another glass of wine?'

But she didn't care to drink very much, and he was driving home.

John was leaning back in his chair and gazing around the pub. He seemed bored. He kept looking over this way but Debbie couldn't see him without turning around. Sandy was fiddling with her phone.

Here came the puddings. He reached for the menu again.

'I'm having Passion Fruit Baked Alaska and yours is the Chocolate Tart with Candied Orange.'

The young couple in the corner were feeding each other their puddings and laughing.

His job had been bearable at first, when it was new and when the weather was good but it was different when it got on to winter. The last few weeks had been cold and the roads icy and he had always been nervous of driving on icy roads. It had been giving him bad dreams lately, dreams about the van going into a skid, dreams about him losing control. He woke up shouting once. Debbie didn't wake, or she didn't say she had anyway.

One day last week it had snowed in the night and the snow had melted on the branches and on the hedges and then frozen again, so there were little droplets of ice like pearls. It should have been beautiful but along with the iciness of the roads it had frightened him. The coldness of it.

The candle was burning low now.

'Shall we go home for our coffee? Go home and sit by the fire?'

But she wanted to sit with John, and with Sandy.

And before he could say anything else, she got up and was walking away.

A Tapestry

Josie heaved the ladder up against the farmhouse wall, gave it a firm shake to test its stability and started to climb, one hand on the ladder and the other holding the bucket of warm soapy water. She was equally at home driving a tractor or delivering a calf, and her strength, along with the boots and baggy green overalls, gave her a somewhat rugged appearance, an effect belied by the wavy dark hair pulled back haphazardly into a band. When she reached the open window she put the bucket on the wide inner sill and turned to look around, pushing back a lock of hair whipped across her face by the brisk south-westerly wind.

She could see all her family's land and over to her cousin's farm and beyond; a complex pattern of undulating fields, hedges and meandering lanes which reached down to the river then up towards the horizon and the dark shadowy bulk of Dartmoor, all laid out like a brightly chequered counterpane in the spring sunshine. Her parents' bungalow and a distant farm on the far side of the river were the only visible dwellings in a landscape that was almost uninhabited, but rich with meaning and memories. That sunken grass-grown lane was the one she and, more recently, her daughter Amy used to follow to reach the school bus. The faint, emerald haze in the Home Field indicated that the fertiliser she had spread in February was working, and the drone of a new John Deere tractor just reaching her on the breeze informed her that her cousin Geoff was ploughing down towards the river.

There was a lightness in the air, an almost imperceptible energy she always associated with the month of March; it was present in the hedgerow trees still grey and bare but charged with a vitality they lacked in winter; it was in the ring of birdsong too after the long silent months, chaffinches singing from the oak by the farm gate and great tits calling 'It's coming, coming, coming'. The bellowing of the cows in the shed seemed subtly different from the resigned sounds of winter, and there was a promise in the clusters of primroses and the shy wild daffodils nestling in the hedgebanks, making her think of Mother's Day, of picking the flowers as a child and being given them as an adult, warm from being clutched in little fingers. Flowers, birds, foxes, deer; she must add details to the website when she had time, but she wouldn't include the badgers, she and Andrew could take no pleasure in their presence.

She could tell by the rattle of metal and the shouted commands to the cows that Andrew was in the big shed. If she held the windowsill and leaned out a little she could see round into the yard where the concrete still gleamed darkly from being hosed down. Two sides were formed by the old stone linhays, solid mid-nineteenth century barns built when the farm was part of the estate and now softened by a jumble of ivy climbing up the rear walls and over the red-tiled roofs. The open-fronted linhays provided storage for a jumble of feed sacks, cans, fertilisers, redundant implements and her father's old Ferguson tractor. The black and white sheepdog, which bore the same name, Shep, as every dog on the farm since her childhood, lay watchfully at the entrance with his nose on his paws. Beyond the old shippon and threshing barn was the huge new cowshed. She scrutinised the shallow inverted V of its steel roof, making a quick calculation of the extent still to be paid for, then she admired the fine pedigree lines of the cows shuffling around the yard in their awkward, bony fashion, knowing instantly their identities and yield. It would not be long before the herd could be put out to graze again and the long winter ritual of scraping out the slurry and strawing down would be over; spring would then have truly arrived, the cows demonstrating through their stiff, frisky canter over the new grass with tails held high that they too felt the change in the air. She watched as one cow moved around restlessly and mounted another. It was the same one she had kept an eye on when she had been milking that morning.

'Andrew! Andrew!'

A stout figure with muck down the front of his overalls appeared from the shed and looked around for her, puzzled at the whereabouts of her voice. He looked quite comical and she hesitated, enjoying his confusion, before waving to attract his attention.

'Here, sweetheart!'

'What be doing up there?'

'Just cleaning windows. That one's bulling, number 312 I think. Yeah, that one.'

He hadn't been in the best mood that morning and grumbled when she told him that their first visitors would arrive later the same day. She had been surprised by the email because although she made sure several weeks ago that the rooms were ready, it was very early in the season and she had not expected any bookings yet, especially at such short notice. But she was delighted, unlike Andrew.

'I'm a farmer not a flippin' tourist attraction! I'm not having 'em stand around watching me milk! And I'm not sitting down to breakfast with 'em either.'

She had known just what he would say and how to placate him. He hadn't been that keen on doing bed and breakfast when she first suggested it back in the autumn so she reassured him that he need hardly see the visitors if that was what he wanted and then she showed him her calculations. When he saw that in a good week in high season the income would almost pay the interest on the bank loan, he went very quiet. It would be worth the inconvenience of always having to do the morning's milking himself.

She hadn't wanted to go back into dairy, not after the foot and mouth. Her gaze travelled reluctantly to the corner of the five acre field below the shed, the area they had fenced off and planted with trees as a memorial. That was the scene of the horror: a nightmare of burning, twisting limbs tended by men in white overalls, the shocking familiarity of black and white markings amidst the carnage, black smoke shutting out the sun and the stench that still haunted them. Afterwards, came the dreadful silence; the deserted fields; Shep lying forlorn in the empty yard, waiting for the cows to return. Josie would have come out of dairy and only kept store cattle and sheep, but she knew that day, when Andrew came in as the cull started and she saw the set of his mouth, that any attempt at persuasion would be wasted.

'Us'll have a better herd than ever, go for real quality, I won't let them buggers drive us out!'

Her father agreed with him, without vehemence but in bewilderment, having milked all his life and not knowing what he would do without it. So they started again and over the years had built up the best herd in the area. Andrew was determined to succeed but could not match the power of the supermarkets when they drove down the price of milk, or the severity of two exceptionally cold winters which forced him to pour the milk down the drain. Josie remembered him being out with the tractor day and night attempting to clear the snow from the long steep lane but the tanker was still unable to reach the farm. It had been a constant struggle but the huge investment in the new shed now precluded any thoughts of coming out of dairy. Josie did all the farm accounts and carefully controlled the release of information to Andrew; a case of mastitis meant withholding the news of increased fertiliser prices; the birth of a fine heifer calf meant she could slip in details of the latest vet's bill. Beneath his brusque exterior he was more sensitive to the burden of responsibility than was Josie; when times were particularly difficult he had bad dreams which woke them both but she would soon go back to sleep. She had experienced losses, early in their marriage, that had thrown mere financial worries into perspective. It was life; you just got on with it.

She turned back to the window, took the dripping sponge from the bucket and pushed it into the corners of the frames where cobwebs gathered below the eaves, then washed down the windows, frames and sill. As she polished the glass with the dry cloth, the room came into view, unfamiliar from this angle so that she saw it as if for the first time, as the visitors would see it. A shaft of sunlight fell on to the stained boards, illuminating the cream, red and blue design of the rug her mother had made. With its sloping ceiling, brass bed and small-paned window the room surely had the character she had claimed for it on the website. A posy of primroses on the bedside table would complete the effect.

It had been her room as a child, and then her daughter Amy's room. Now Amy was away at university for much of the year; when she returned she would have a room at the far end of the corridor, next to Andrew and Josie, leaving this end for visitors. There was a new bathroom and then another letting bedroom, with the possibility of doing up her parents' old room if there was demand for a third. Her parents had moved into the bungalow following the death of her grandmother last year. Josie supposed she and Andrew would move there one day, if her wishes were fulfilled and Amy moved back to the farm and had a family.

She had worked hard all winter to make the rooms ready. When her hours at the health centre were reduced, the twenty-five mile round trip was no longer viable; she recognised she would miss the opportunity for human contact that her job had afforded and knew at once what she wanted to do. She rapidly made plans, studying the websites of other farm B&B's and visualising the renewal of the dilapidated rooms. The visitors could have their own separate entrance through the rarely used front door and could have breakfast in the dining room, now fresh and bright after decades of being used as a musty storeroom for drifts of old papers, piles of Farmer's Weekly and cardboard boxes full of Christmas decorations. The sense of anticipation she felt now that all her efforts were coming to fruition gave her an energy equal to the vitality she sensed in the March air.

She descended the ladder, moved it over to the next window and positioned the base just inside the stone edge of the overgrown flower bed. There was an old house martin's nest close to this window, a neat convex mud cup magically fixed under the eaves. She hoped that when the birds returned and performed their aerial acrobatics before sweeping down like arrows into their nests, the visitors would be charmed rather than disturbed by their loud chattering. She leaned in through the window to rest the bucket on the windowsill and caught sight of a reflection in her grandmother's dressing table mirror. She saw a broad, ruddy face with a streak of mud on one cheek, a rather large nose and untidy dark hair.

'Goodness me, what a sight!'

She rubbed away the mud and smiled at the mirror.

'Good afternoon, welcome to the farm! Did you have a pleasant journey?'

The reflection did not engender confidence. She would have to tidy herself up or the visitors might turn right around and go back where they came from. She pictured a vase of wild daffodils on the dressing table and remembered being fascinated as a child to see their number doubled by their mirror image. Now that the evenings were beginning to draw out, it was probable that it would still be light when the visitors arrived. She imagined them admiring the daffodils and standing at the open window, sensing from the expectant stillness in the air and the undefinable quality of light that spring was almost here.

She washed down the window then polished the glass until it offered a gleaming reflection of the patterned fields and pockets of dark woodland. A movement caught her eye and she turned carefully on the ladder to see her mother in wellingtons and with an apron beneath her jacket making her way from the bungalow, hurrying along with short, quick steps interspersed with small leaps as she dodged the puddles on the rough surface of the lane. She was holding a plastic carrier bag.

'Mum! Yoo-hoo!'

Josie descended the ladder and met her mother as she came through the farm gate holding up the bag for inspection, her habitual calm expression broken by an eager smile. Josie had phoned her with the good news as soon as the email arrived.

'I was just going to come down to you, Mum. Do you want to come to the supermarket after dinner? There's some bits I need to get and can you plant some polyanthus if I buy them for the garden?'

They looked over the wall at the little garden overgrown with rosettes of dandelion leaves and a few desiccated brambles.

'There now! I know just how it should look!' Her mother flourished the carrier bag again. 'See what I've brought for 'ee, 'tis just the thing for the visitors. Come on in the kitchen and have a look.'

Josie moved the kettle over to boil on the Aga and cleared a pile of papers from the large kitchen table. Her mother carefully removed a framed picture from the bag.

'Now, do you remember this?'

Behind the fly-spotted glass was an embroidery on cream-coloured fabric. It was immediately apparent that the long, white house depicted in careful stitches was the farmhouse in which they stood. They could see the row of five upstairs windows that Josie had been cleaning, the little garden with its grey stone wall and a rambling rose around the front door, and a black and white sheepdog lying with his nose on his paws outside the kitchen entrance through which they had just passed. There were the linhays containing piles of logs or perhaps turnips and, in the foreground, chickens pecking in the yard and several horned Red Devon cows waiting patiently to be milked.

'It's Great Grandma's tapestry, I haven't seen it for years!'

It had hung on her grandmother's bedroom wall when Josie was a child but was put away for the move to the bungalow and had remained in the back of a wardrobe ever since. Below the picture was embroidered the name of the farm and the date, March 1924.

'There, that was when they bought the farm from the estate,' said Josie's mother, 'She was so proud to know that they'd bought it, you see, that she did all this work.'

'How ever did she find the time to learn that sort of thing?'

'Well, she wasn't born to a farm life you see, just married into it, so she'd learned to be clever like that when she was young. And she used to do her sewing when she was sitting in the market on a Tuesday selling her cream and butter and that. But she didn't keep it up when time went on. Look at it now! You couldn't buy anything like that how ever much you paid.'

'I'll clean it up and we can hang it in the dining room. That's where it should be, so's the visitors can look at it while they eat their breakfast. We've a photo of great grandma too, haven't we, that I can put up alongside?'

They pored over the detail again. 'The flowers are poppies, put there to remember her brother who died at the Somme, that's what my mother told me. They shouldn't be out in March of course, not really. And that's the same rose that's there today or one like it, surely.'

Josie straightened up and went to make coffee.

'That's what we'll do then! We can buy some poppy seeds and give the rose some manure and just buy some polyanthus to brighten it up for the time being. Pity we haven't got the old red cows really!'

'Grandmother used to do all the milking by hand. 'Twas marvellous, when you come to think of it. Course they didn't give the milk that the Friesians do but it was better for cream.'

They sat with their coffee after Josie had carried mugs out to Andrew and her father in the shed. Josie had never known her great grandmother but her mother was flushed with excitement at the memories the tapestry had brought back. It was agreed that she had been a remarkable woman and had a clarity of vision and a determination to succeed that had overcome her husband's more cautious approach. It was she who had resolved to make the change from horses to the first tractor and to use the new fertilisers. Josie fetched her photograph from the dining room and there she was, staring rather self-consciously back at them as she stood outside the back door, her short dark hair curling unfashionably over her ears, her arm linked with her husband's. He looked even more embarrassed and seemed to be squeezed uncomfortably into his best suit.

Josie's mother sighed with satisfaction.

'There, just look at her! 'Tis a shame we can't tell her about the bed and breakfast. She'd be so proud of you, Josie.'

By late afternoon Josie had put the finishing touches to the bedrooms, hung the tapestry in the dining room, washed the best china for breakfast and arranged the cereals on a side table. On returning from the supermarket, her mother had planted polyanthus and sown poppy seeds while Josie fed the calves. When she went back into the house to change her clothes, the phone was ringing; it was another booking for bed and breakfast, for two nights the following weekend. In her excitement she sent Amy a text then grabbed her mother around the waist and waltzed her around the kitchen, ignoring her pleas to 'Mind my corns!' until they both fell laughing on to the sofa.

When Andrew came in for a cup of tea she reminded him about the visitors' imminent arrival.

'Should I get changed do you think?' He looked quite anxious and she stroked his hair with affection while surreptitiously pulling out a piece of straw.

'No, you'll do. Have your tea and I'll have a sweep up outside and look out for the car.'

The sun was low in the sky, suffusing the feathered clouds with pink and reflecting on to the white walls of the farmhouse. In the cool late afternoon air above the Home Field a skylark voiced its liquid warbling refrain. The sound took her back to her childhood when she used to wonder how it could manage to sing for so long without drawing breath; today she felt she could do the same and if she managed to fly too, it would scarcely surprise her. She had more plans; a wind turbine to decrease their fuel bills, a trial of a new clover blend and a proposition for Amy that just might bring her back to the farm. She quickly swept the paved area where the visitors would park their car and as she finished she saw a car turn the corner and start to climb the steep lane towards the farm.

'Andrew, Andrew! It's coming!'

And she hurriedly put away the broom, smoothed her hair and smiled in anticipation as the car approached the farm gate, ready to greet the next challenge.

The Arrival

Derek looked out of the low cottage window at the village square lying tranquil in the April sunshine. The cottages surrounding the Square were of diverse stature and their individual windows lent expressions of hostility, caution or welcome as they awaited a burst of activity which never materialised. Derek watched as Mrs Davy's ginger cat wandered between the parked cars, paused in the empty road and lay down, stretching and rolling on the tarmac.

Derek's cottage was in the narrower part of the Square and just a few doors down to his left it narrowed still further until it became a lane, which led in turn to the main road. Turn right for Crediton, that was what he said to visitors. Not that he had many visitors.

Mrs Davy came into view, stepping out from her doorway on his right to have a better look at the house across the road. Today they had a common interest, a rare occurrence. The house had been a focus of attention in the village ever since old John Gilbert had died. The landlord, who had never found it necessary to install an indoor toilet during the fifty years that John had rented the cottage, had moved in a team of builders and before long an advert appeared in the local paper, offering the house 'fully renovated, no expense spared' at a rent that would have astounded John. Today, the carpet fitters had arrived and Derek watched as they came out to their van carrying a roll of carpet between them. It was said in the village that a foreign family was going to move in and Derek was not alone in feeling a lack of enthusiasm at the prospect.

Mrs Davy walked stiffly across the road to the men. Her hip was playing her up again.

'They'm coming then. They'm moving in soon.'

Derek moved away from the window and carried his coffee out into the back garden. He sat on the bench near the

31

hedge and stared at the weed-grown vegetable plot. Perhaps he would grass it over this year.

He had moved to the village from Exeter because it seemed the sort of place that would not change and, as his marriage had just ended bitterly after nearly thirty years, he felt he had had about as much change as he could take. When he first drove into the village he saw a herd of Friesians grazing in a meadow with a spreading oak tree and was reminded of the carefully arranged figures in the toy farm he had played with as a boy; a horse, cows, a farmer with a wooden staff and a milkmaid on a stool. The docile cows and the thick-walled cottage in the peaceful square made him think he was coming to a gentler, more innocent place, the old England of his childhood, but his initial impressions proved to be inaccurate. He learnt that the cows were milked automatically in a huge shed attended by Polish youths being paid less than the minimum wage and, soon after he moved in, a new estate was built on the meadow and a pool table installed in the old thatched pub to accommodate all the teenagers with London accents.

He wandered up the paved path that ran between the lawn and the vegetable plot. Bees hummed over the dandelion flowers and a chaffinch called from the lilac tree, a repetitive jangle like a bunch of keys being rattled. He turned to look south, over the roof of the cottage to the expansive fields and woods of mid-Devon and the hazy bulk of Dartmoor in the distance. There was exuberance in the air, a sense that something was going to happen, but he did not feel that it had anything to do with him. In his garden the grass needed cutting and the weeds were growing almost visibly now that this warm weather had followed the showers and he knew he really should do some work on it. It would be good for him; he had been told he should take regular exercise. He had to go to Exeter that afternoon for his second appointment with the cardiologist. The hospital waiting-room would be full of fearful middle-aged people like himself, staring at the relentlessly cheerful presenters on the television screen which occupied one wall, and the thought sucked away whatever pleasure he might have found in his spring garden.

The drone of a tractor drifted on the breeze along with the pungent smell of muck-spreading. From the Square came the sound of van doors being slammed and an engine starting up. The carpet fitters had finished then. It was said that the tenants of John Gilbert's cottage were going to open an Indian takeaway to replace the old burger bar on the small industrial estate on the outskirts of the village.

'Of course, you know they'm Muslims,' Mrs Davy had told him with a challenging stare, as if daring him to deny that the appearance of a suicide bomber in the Square was now inevitable. He'd heard a woman in the post office declare that she had left London in order to be away from 'people like that', while kinder souls had said the newcomers would be made welcome whatever their colour or religion. For himself, he felt a sense of regret at what seemed to be a break with the village's past, a rupture in the connection between the cheerful harvesters brandishing scythes in the old photographs and the tractor driver who waved as he passed today; the line that he could himself trace on his family tree, leading from the nineteenth century Devon labourers down through the generations to the shopkeepers, the mechanics, the engineer, himself. Where did a dark-skinned face fit into these images? The thought was immediately followed by a pang of guilt as he imagined the look of disdain on his son's face, accompanied by the cutting, dismissive words he knew to be entirely deserved.

A whisper and a giggle came from the other side of his garden wall and he turned, immediately watchful. A branch of the old lilac tree grew horizontally out from the gnarled trunk, along the top of the wall and down towards the path that ran between the gardens. It provided an irresistible temptation to children who used the path to reach the village playground and he frequently saw a face grinning at him from the higher branches of the tree. He crept closer and stood near the wall, waiting until a head appeared. The fair-haired boy with a plump face was looking down to find his next foothold and Derek took several quick steps forward, undetected.

'OUT! This is private property! How many times have I got to tell you?'

The boy nearly fell from the tree in shock then dropped quickly back into the lane and Derek heard giggles and two pairs of feet running up the path. He really must do something about cutting the branch back, but the thought of the awkward sawing made him feel weary. He sat down again. Perhaps he should get someone to remove the branch for him. He did not want to be forever chasing the children away. He berated himself for having become old and ill-tempered, but the fact remained that he did not want the children in his garden. He didn't even know how to talk to his own grandchildren.

When his wife had left him, his son had been solicitous for a while but sympathy had made Derek feel uncomfortable; he was accustomed to being the one to hand out advice and understanding, not the one to receive it. When his son and daughter-in-law visited, the difficulty of having to cook them a meal and to talk to them without anyone beside him to ask the important questions made the absence of his wife even harder to bear and when the grandchildren came along he did not know how to play with them in the way she would have done. The visits ended in awkward silences and earlier than planned departures, and in time they became much less frequent. His son still phoned him occasionally but rarely visited. He had a young family to keep him occupied; he would not want to be bothered with his father's health problems and old-fashioned attitudes.

It was April, so wasn't his grandson's birthday at the end of the month? The other one, the baby, was born in the winter. He must check his diary and buy a card. He was not very good at keeping at touch but he would buy his grandson a card. And perhaps a present. He did not know what children liked these days but it could not be too hard to buy a present for a five-year-old boy.

He heard a different bird call, a quick, liquid chirruping, and he looked up. A bluish-black bird with slender wings and a fast, easy flight swooped over the garden and turned quickly to soar up again, singing all the while. A swallow! The first this year, all the way from Africa. He shaded his eyes to watch it. Back and forth it flew, now in a looping figure of eight against the blue sky, now in a wide circle, always returning to fly over the garden until it landed suddenly on the roof of his shed. It stopped singing and stared at him. He stared back. The shed, really a small barn, was at the end of the garden but despite the distance he could make out the bird's creamy breast and rust-red throat, the long forked tail resting on the tiles. Suddenly the bird rose again, wheeled around and flew through the open upper door of the shed. He had never seen swallows go in there before. Within a few seconds it was out again, flying low over the hedges then up and away. He walked up the garden and peered over the door into the gloom.

The clinic was running an hour late. There had been a downpour as Derek walked from the hospital car park and his trousers were still damp. He shifted uncomfortably in his seat and tried to concentrate on the car magazine on his lap, but the over-enthusiastic voices from the television screen distracted him. It must surely be his turn next. The afternoon had not gone well so far; there had been roadworks in Newton St Cyres and then such an interminable crawl through Exeter he feared he would be really late. He looked up at the clock again; a woman smiled sympathetically at him and he hastily turned away. Suddenly the door of the consulting room flew open and the man with the shaved head who had been fidgeting and complaining in the waiting area strode out, pausing in the doorway to shout.

'And I'll not be told what to do by a black bastard like you!' He turned and glared at the crowded room. 'Bastards should go back to the jungle where they belong!'

He disappeared through the exit, punching the wall with his fist as he went. There was a shocked silence as every single person sat rigidly staring at the door, then the receptionist lifted the phone and Derek caught the word 'security' in her urgent whisper. The plump, cheerful nurse coming out from the consulting room broke the spell.

'That won't do his heart condition any good! Now then, Mr Green, please!'

Derek rose and crossed the room, feeling every eye on him. As the nurse closed the door he heard the whispering and the shocked exclamations starting.

Dr Badero rose from his seat, smiled and shook Derek's hand. His expression was calm and welcoming.

'So, Mr Green, how are you feeling?'

Derek fumbled for his words. The pain had gone, he said, he could walk a little further but still got tired; he had felt a little nauseous but that had passed now.

'You're still not smoking? That's good, well done!' That wide smile again. He went through the results of the ECG, running his finger up and down the jagged lines, elaborating on their significance and explaining why they indicated that an angiogram would not be necessary at present. Derek strained to follow the unfamiliar intonation in the precise, expressive voice.

'So, keep taking your medication, take some gentle exercise and, of course, no more cigarettes please! You can then have a long and active life and no more worries. Now, any questions?' Derek shook his head and then hesitated. He still felt somewhat shaken.

'I'm sorry Doctor, about what happened.... Here in England, it shouldn't....'

Dr Badero rose and patted him on the arm; that smile again.

'Well, it occurs from time to time unfortunately, we get used to it, you know.'

By the end of the week there were two swallows. Derek watched from the bench as they raced above the garden, wheeling, turning and chasing with such agility it was hard to keep track of them. First one, then the other turned sharply at the top of the garden and shot through the open door of the shed. He heard the lilting, liquid song from inside and then the birds dashed out again and one landed on the washing line, lightly balancing, its glossy dark blue back and long tail streamers catching the sun. It was enchanting, swallows in his own shed! As a boy on his uncle's farm, he had loved to lie in the sweet-smelling hay and watch as they flew into the thatched barn to land for a second on the edge of one of the nests on the rafters, eliciting the frantic chirruping of the hungry young, then out again as fast as thought. He leaned back on the bench. And was he not well? Dr Badero had told him so. Since his appointment in Exeter he had felt a dark cloud of anxiety beginning to lift; he had become so accustomed to it, he had hardly recognised its existence.

He walked to the end of the garden and opened the shed door. It was a stable door; it was fortunate he had forgotten to close the top half last week. Already he could see the beginnings of a nest up in the corner, and a slew of bird droppings and wisps of dried grass down over the expensive upholstered garden chairs he stored below. He did not want to risk disturbing the swallows by moving things around so he took some old plastic sacks and draped them over the chairs. He saw that they had been perching on an old length of wire which was strung across from the rafters. One end was rather rusty and he secured it with a piece of string so that it would not break and fall.

The next day the new family moved in. Derek watched from the window as the unfamiliar car was parked and the occupants got out, looking around uneasily until the man pointed out the cottage. The woman wore bright blue trousers and a long matching tunic but the man and the two children, a boy and a girl, were wearing what looked to Derek like quite ordinary clothes. Their black hair gleamed in the afternoon sun, an exotic contrast to the washed out colours of the cob cottages around the Square. When the door closed behind them, he imagined them in John Gilbert's dilapidated front room; but, of course, it was all different now. It wasn't like that now.

Later, a furniture van arrived. Derek guessed that Mrs Davy was watching from behind her curtains.

The swallows completed the nest. When Derek peered tentatively in through the open door he could just see the tail feathers of one bird protruding from the meticulously crafted cradle on the rafters and guessed that she was sitting on eggs. In the mornings, he watched until he saw a bird fly out before hurrying in to remove the lawn mower, the trowel or whatever else he might need that day, so as not to disturb her.

One morning when he wandered out into the garden after breakfast, both birds were flying repeatedly in and out of the shed uttering shrill alarm calls, chis-*ick*! chis-*ick*! chis-*ick*! He watched them. Their calls intensified as he approached the door but their focus of attention was not on him but on something inside the shed. He looked over the door. Crouched threateningly on the floor, looking up at the swallows that continued to dart in and out of the door past Derek's head, was Mrs Davy's ginger cat.

'Get out!'

He opened the door and the cat fled, helped along by a kick that was only just intended to miss. He stood back. One swallow flew back into the shed and the other, the alarm calls diminishing, watched from the washing line. He would have to do something. The cat would catch the young when they fluttered from the nest, even if it did not catch one of the adults. He looked at his watch; he was due at a social group meeting in Crediton in an hour and a half. He went into the shed, moving quietly, and the swallow remained on the nest. At the back he found an old piece of plastic guttering, then he picked up his saw and set to work.

He returned contented from Crediton. The meeting was something to look forward to each month; he liked to have a drink at the bar with the other men before the lunch and the talk. The friends he met there also had mild health problems and occasional scares; they too found the modern world difficult to comprehend and the future dark; together they felt vindicated in grumbling about the present and dwelling on their successful pasts. Standing around the bar with his small group of friends, he had told the story of how he had first started working for Post Office Telephones, of the time when he was promoted although he had less experience than others, and the minutiae of the changes over the years. He had, as he told it, felt himself to be significant again.

He had told them also about his new neighbours. He was tentative in expressing his sentiments about tradition and belonging but even so, the carefully chosen words would not, he knew, have been approved of by his son. He felt even more uncomfortable when others spoke more vehemently, about the shortage of work for the 'locals' and the crime statistics, and he knew his son would have been angry and would have felt he should not mix with people who held such views.

He had seen one of his new neighbours in the post office. When she came in he had already been served and was looking at the handwritten advertisements on the notice board. She wore a vivid green outfit and was beautiful; she looked out of place in the rundown post office. He had not said hello, but would have done had she looked at him. The other customers had not greeted her either but Brenda the postmistress had been friendly and had asked her how she was settling in and she had responded shyly, her English a little difficult to understand. There had been sardonic comments after she left.

He took his cup of tea out to the garden seat, feeling in need of some fresh air after the closeness of the room in Crediton. The first flowers were opening on the lilac, and the scent reminded him of his grandmother's garden. He had once picked some blossoms from her tree but she had told him that it should never be brought indoors lest the sweet scent should attract fairies, which might then steal him from his bed and take him away. He had half-believed it, being a more naïve child than he imagined today's children must be. His friends in Crediton told him how their grandchildren occupied themselves and of their sophistication with modern technology. He sat back on the seat. His hedge was greening up nicely, more leaves opening every day to shield him from Mrs Davy's gaze. As he relaxed he saw her ginger cat creeping along the base of the far hedge and he sat very still to watch. It slunk around the top of the vegetable plot, its belly close to the ground, and when it reached the shed it gathered itself and sprung up on to the lower door. Instantly there was a commotion and a loud clatter as something fell on to the path, tangling with the cat which leapt free with a yowl and streaked back across the garden and disappeared through the hedge. Derek slapped his knee and laughed out loud. The swallow shot back and forth over the garden expressing its alarm.

'Don't worry; he won't do that again in a hurry, once more at the most, I would say. You'll be safe now.'

He walked up to the shed and replaced the piece of guttering over the lower door. As he did so he heard childish voices from the far side of the lilac tree. Was he to be invaded from every side? Well, he had frightened off the cat and would frighten off the children, once and for all.

He moved stealthily towards the lilac. There was a rustling and then a small, high voice.

'I'll get up first. If I get through I'll help you, all right?'

He was poised, ready, with his hand raised; he would teach them a lesson they would not forget. Suddenly, a head appeared and he saw clear brown skin, dark pools for eyes, gleaming blue-black hair. Derek froze; a moment's breath, then he brought his hand slowly down to his side. The boy saw him and his face lit up.

'Hello! I didn't know anyone was there! Did you hear me coming up the tree?'

The boy climbed up a little further to sit on a branch and he gazed out over the garden, his face framed by clusters of lilac, then he looked down at Derek again who was mesmerised by the bright, guileless eyes, as shiny as blackcurrants.

'Is this your garden? Do you live here? Can I help my sister up?'

Then the boy was leaning down through the tree, as lithe as a gymnast, and reaching down to his sister.

'Come on! Hold my hand and I'll pull you up.'

And then there were two of them sitting side by side on the branch with the lilac flowers resting on their hair. Derek did not know what to say. The words that came to him sounded ungracious, and they looked so beautiful sitting there in the tree smiling at him, like butterflies that would take flight at the least provocation.

'What's your name?'

The boy was looking directly at him, almost challenging him. The girl was more shy but continued to smile at him, leaning close to her brother.

'Derek.' He had almost said Mr Green. 'And yours?'

'Salim. And my sister's called Haseena. I'm seven. She's only five but she'll be seven one day. Have you got any children we can play with?'

'No, no children.' How ridiculous to feel ill at ease with this charming boy. 'At least, not here. I have a grown-up son, and grandchildren of about your age.'

'We want some children to play with, that's why we were going to the playground. My father took us there yesterday but I know the way now.'

His gaze travelled around the garden as if he expected to find some children hiding amongst the shrubs or below the steps that led to the back door. The little girl had her finger in her mouth and gazed at him with those huge dark eyes.

'Your mother won't know where you are. She'll be worried about you, won't she?'

'No, not unless we're late. We have to be back by five o'clock and it's - ,' the boy stared at his watch with great concentration, 'it's twenty-five past four.'

'Oh, I see.'

'Is that your house as well?' The boy was pointing at the shed.

'No. No, it's not a house.'

'What is it, then?'

'It's a shed, a barn.' He hesitated. 'Actually there's something in there you might like to see. Some birds. But first, shall we go and tell your mother where you are?'

It was a big drop, from the lilac tree down into the garden.

'Shall I help you down?'

One by one he lifted the children down from the tree and with the sensation of their firm, light bodies propelled trustingly into his hands came a rush of long-forgotten memories; the love and warmth that had emanated from his own child, his eager face, the joy of his company.

Together they went through the house and out into the Square. It was deserted, and the cottages stood by and watched. He took the children's hands to cross the road and he knocked on the door of John Gilbert's old cottage. The woman came to the door and was surprised, looking from him to the children. Quickly he explained how they came to be with him, and that he wanted to show them some birds that were nesting in his shed and would like her to come as well. He talked too fast and had to repeat his words again, remembering to smile; he wanted very much to seem welcoming. He could see past her into the front room; a light carpet, cream paint on the walls, a large leather sofa. She was hesitant but agreed to come and together they walked across to Derek's house.

As they approached the shed he spoke in a whisper.

'There! There's one swallow on the roof. Do you see it?'
The woman picked up the little girl and pointed out the
bird.

'They come all the way from Africa every spring to nest
here in England. Now, look inside.'

They spoke in whispers as he pointed out the grassy nest
on the rafters and the dark blue head and long forked tail that
protruded from it, then he lifted Salim up so he could have a
better look. He told them how the eggs would hatch and the
parents would fly in and out all day bringing flies for the little
ones until the day came when they would flutter from the nest
and then suddenly fly out of the door and up into the sky,
soaring and wheeling like their parents. As the swallow took
off from the roof as if to demonstrate, the woman gasped in
recognition and told him that there were very similar birds at
her parents' house in Bangladesh and they were thought to
bring good fortune.

'You must come and see them again. Perhaps - you could
bring your husband, have a cup of tea.'

The woman told him he was very kind. She said that they
wanted to get to know people in the village and to make
friends, but it was hard, moving to a place where they knew
no one. They walked back through the garden and Salim
slipped his hand into Derek's.

He stood in the doorway and watched as they crossed the
Square, turning to wave when they reached their front door.
He could sense Mrs Davy at her window. He went back into
his house and stared at his living room. It looked drab and the
air was stale; he really must open some windows. He ran his
finger along the windowsill and saw a clear line in the grime.
If he was going to have visitors for tea, he would have to
make the house look more inviting. Well, he could do that.

The sensation of Salim's hand in his had reminded him of
a walk long ago when his son had been small. They were
walking up a long hill from the coast where they had spent the
afternoon and the child was tired so he had told him a story as
they walked. He couldn't remember now what it was about

but it had held his son enthralled, and when Derek paused for breath he had pulled at his hand, pleading with him to continue.

He had had no trouble talking to children then.

He pulled a dusty album of old photographs from the bookshelf and sat down.

Later he went upstairs and looked at the bedrooms and saw that the two spare rooms could be decorated, he could buy a new bed for his son and daughter-in-law and there was enough space for bunk beds in the smaller room. Then he went out into the garden again. The light was dimming, there was a pink glow in the sky to the west and the scent of lilac filled the garden. The weeds on the vegetable plot were higher than ever but it would not take long to clear them and it was the right time of year for laying turf. There was room for a swing, perhaps a slide or a climbing frame as well. When his family came to stay Salim and Haseena could visit and all the children could play together. The swallow was perched on the washing line, swaying easily to keep its balance. Soon there would be little ones flying out of the stable door and away into the open sky and they would return home to roost each evening, three or four sitting close together on the wire below the rafters.

He addressed the swallow.

'And you'll return every year, won't you?'

And he walked back through the fragrant garden to telephone his son.

The Tarka Line

Soon after the train drew out of Exeter St David's, there was a sudden, surprising smell that permeated every inch of the two small carriages, causing the passengers to turn to each other and pull faces and smile, and Jessica knew that she was nearly home.

'Muckspreading,' she said to Chris, 'like they've just done the first cut of silage. It's to make the grass grow again.'

'Will it smell like that on your farm?'

'It might.'

They held each other's gaze, smiling, then she looked down at their intertwined hands, tanned from the afternoon they had spent lying together in St James's Park, and she rubbed her thumb slowly along the back of his hand. Of course it would be all right – how could she have thought it might not? She'd left London behind and was here, suddenly, on a little train swaying through a lush green valley with Chris, whose finger gently traced the circuit of her knee through the fabric of her trousers. It seemed like something she'd long been promised, being grown-up at last perhaps. Through the open window came a warm, late afternoon breeze and snatches of birdsong, just audible above the din of the engine as it rattled past hawthorn trees laden with blossom and sloping fields grazed by well-grown lambs.

On the train between Paddington and Exeter she had been afraid that the journey was a mistake. The morning had dragged as she sat confined in the office, obliged to keep still on the plastic chair and concentrate on the screen but constantly disturbed by the persistent energy that rose from deep inside her and by thoughts of Chris, his physical presence, the sound of his voice and the smell of his skin which was like a clean sheet drying in the wind. When three o'clock came she ran down the stairs and out on to the dusty

London street, counting down the minutes until she would see him.

He too had left work early so that they could meet at the station and although he had held her for a long moment before they hurried to get on board, she sensed that he was anxious about the work he had left unfinished. The Friday train was full of people with blank faces and they had sat opposite a grey-looking man from whom emanated the sickly-sweet smell of alcohol, engulfing them for the entire journey and making her feel nauseous. They had sat in silence and after a while Chris started to write work emails on his phone while she gazed out of the window or pretended to read. Sealed behind tinted glass and chilly from the air-conditioning, she had looked out as the high-speed train streaked past flat fields grazed by severely shorn sheep and stations bound by utilitarian steel railings beyond which row upon row of vehicles waited in car parks. It was only when they reached Exeter and stepped out into air that was rich with the scent of newly-mown grass, that they talked, sitting close together on a bench at the far end of the platform in the gentle May sunshine, sharing a bar of chocolate and an over-sized paper cup of coffee while they waited for the Barnstaple train to arrive.

She watched him as he gazed out of the window. It was the combination of composure and vitality that had first attracted her. She had seen him singing and playing guitar in the bar down the road when she called in with her housemates and watched as he poured emotion into the words. Everyone had listened while he sang but when he came to the bar, shy without his guitar, it was Jessica he spoke to. Like her, he had finished university a year ago and had come to London in pursuit of work. He had been less fortunate than she and after one short-term contract, was now in an internship at the publishers of a music journal, but was optimistic about being taken on permanently and in the meantime made some money singing in pubs and bars.

He put his arm around her and she wriggled closer, feeling the warmth of his body through his shirt.

'Will it be your mum or your dad who comes to meet us at the station?'

'Probably my mum. Dad will still be milking.'

What would he think of her family? Her parents were so busy on the farm that they had little awareness of the world beyond their 400 acres and the social scene at Holsworthy market and did not realise how unusual their lives were. They would talk about nitrates directives and flying herds with little sense of their audience, her father lapsing into an even broader accent in his exasperation with the Environment Agency and her brother enthusing about the latest antics of the Young Farmers, interests she used to be able to share. This evening they would eat at the kitchen table, moving piles of papers out of the way to accommodate the extra guest, and her father would hurry out while finishing the last mouthful to attend to a calving or continue with the silaging. It was all very different from Chris's home.

The scent of newly-cut grass replaced the smell of muck. She leaned forward to watch a Claas forage harvester edging its way around a field alongside a tractor and trailer and she made a quick assessment of the depth of cut grass. The farmer would be satisfied with his first cut. She was back on familiar ground and sure of all she saw, quite unlike her experience of London where so many sights were perplexing, even after a year.

In the next field was a herd of beautiful dark red cows with curly forelocks and very young calves by their sides.

'What sort of cows are those then, Farmer Jess?'

'Red Rubies, they're Devon cattle. They're raised for beef mainly. We have Friesians, they're best for milk.'

'My Devon lass,' he whispered and his lips brushed the lobe of her ear, tickling her, and she pushed him away laughing.

She had visited his parents' home for the first time a few weeks previously. His old school friend was having a party and he asked her to go with him. This weekend they were to visit her friend's first sculpture exhibition. Those were the spoken reasons for the visits. Chris's parents lived in a large detached house just outside Worcester and were interested in the arts and current affairs and had carefully considered opinions which they discussed around the beautifully laid dining table. *His* mother was neatly elegant, so unlike her mother who lived in wellingtons and struggled with her weight. They had made her very welcome, had asked sensible questions about her job and had kissed her affectionately when it was time to leave for London.

'You weren't too bored, were you?' he had said on the way back. He spoke carelessly but his eyes, full of apprehension, gave him away. She reassured him and warned that the visit to her parents would be different but he had just laughed, saying he wouldn't mind if they set him to work. She was sure he didn't realise how mechanised the farm was and rather feared he imagined throwing corn to free-range hens or bottle-feeding lambs.

The train clanked and swayed, throwing her against Chris's shoulder, and she let her head rest against him as she looked out of the window. The glass in this carriage was not tinted and everything looked new and impossibly green in the spring sunshine; the acid green of new oak leaves, the vivid lime and dark copper of the beeches, everything alive and growing. The engine shrieked a friendly warning and they clattered over a level crossing where a couple of cars and a Land Rover waited in a deep leafy lane and a child's hand waved from a car window. She imagined standing in the lane when the train and the cars had passed, hearing the engines dying away and being replaced by the tiny sounds of small creatures deep in the hedge, the whispering loveliness of new leaves in the breeze and the song of a blackbird or thrush. She had walked for miles through such lanes, to and from the school bus or a friend's house, and they were present in her dreams with their high sheltering banks and gateways with sudden distant vistas. Recently, at work, she had been asked to design a bank to shelter an urban footpath and almost without thinking had drawn on her deep familiarity with Devon hedgebanks, but no careful planting scheme could achieve the effect of centuries of haphazard growth. She spent her days entering precise details measured in millimetres into a computer in order to create environments suitable for work or relaxation, yet her childhood surroundings were naturally more perfect that anything she could construct. Chris had never been to Devon and she really hoped that he would like it. He was sitting up quite straight and she watched his eyes flicking back and forth as new vistas appeared from the train, and she admired the curve of his brow and his dark lashes. She squeezed his hand.

'So, what do you think of Devon so far?'

'It looks like an advert for a holiday,' he said, 'amazing, the thatched cottages and the lanes and the river. Wow, look at that house! You could sit at the end of the garden with your feet in the river and no one around to see, except us on the train.

Is that farm anything like yours?' He pointed to an immaculate thatched house with a small barn and a row of stables.

'No, that's not a working farm anymore. It's...'

She tried to visualise her childhood home as he might see it.

'The house is old, but there are like – well, it's all much bigger than that, and messier. Lots of modern buildings around the old farmhouse, a big open barn, all steel, for the cows in winter. The milking parlour, that's very high-tech. I guess it looks more like a factory in some ways except there's always the sound and smell of the cows. And the fields around, the land, that's beautiful.'

She pictured it as she described it and felt a rush of affection for her home, for the warmth of the kitchen, the smells of the yard and bellowing of the cows and for the fields which had been her playground. The train click-clacked rhythmically on the rails, chanting the refrain familiar from so many of her journeys from university and then from work: I'm go-ing home, I'm go-ing home.

Chris gazed at her as she spoke. Every emotion she felt was played out on her face and in her expressive dark eyes; he never tired of looking at her. Sometimes he made himself look away and out of the window, afraid that she might find his constant attention irritating.

The landscape he could see was almost as beautiful and natural as Jess, as though it were the ground from which she had grown. He felt he had never truly appreciated the countryside before, but then everything had felt new and different in the three months since they met. He never tired of her company. He loved her spontaneity, her sensuous beauty, her occasional forthright opinions uttered with the hint of a Devon accent, her limitless good nature.

He felt uneasy about the forthcoming evening. He supposed they would sit and talk to her parents and they were bound to ask questions, about his job and his ambitions. It probably would not sound like proper work to them. Not like growing food, producing milk - what could be more important than that? He didn't know anything about farming. He would probably ask ridiculous questions. Jess would think he was stupid. On the journey from Paddington she had been very quiet, probably wishing she had never asked him.

Last weekend in St James's Park he had thought he was in heaven. He had taken her hand as they walked across the grass towards the shade of an old oak and marvelled at the soft curve of her palm and the warm resonance of her voice when she laughed. They shared a picnic of ciabatta, black olives, ripe cherry tomatoes and an avocado dip that he had made himself and both made appreciative noises until they made each other laugh. He poured chilled wine into glasses - he had deliberated endlessly between wine and cans of lager - and they sat with their backs to the oak and exchanged stories of their childhoods and teenage years, laughing at the anxieties and embarrassing misconceptions now truly left behind. Jess talked about her work and he heard the passion in her voice alongside the frustration at the constrictions placed on her and for the first time he confessed his hopes of freelancing and developing his music. Then she lay down with her head in his lap and her hand resting on his hip; he stroked her hair and gazed down at her half-closed eyelids and parted lips and felt that the world had never been so full of wonder.

He had numerous half-formed plans stretching into a colourful future, every aspect of which included Jess. A holiday that summer, just the two of them together, camping in Dorset if it was fine or taking the Eurostar to France and alighting hand-in-hand whenever the fancy took them. He dreamt of lying together on a sandy beach secluded by cliffs and swimming out to a small deserted island; of climbing Scafell Pike on a glisteningly bright winter's day; of relaxing on a sofa in a bright bay-windowed flat that seemed to be their own. He had started to do some research and tentatively plan how and when these glorious events might take place. He had yet to mention the schemes to Jess but he would, soon. Perhaps this weekend he could casually mention a holiday. He might also sing her the song he had written for her, but as he watched her now, looking out at the landscape that had helped to form her, he thought he might need to rewrite the refrain. He could include this amazing little train, the repetitive clacking of its wheels; di dah di dah, di dah di dah; what was it they were saying?

Chris was quiet. Jessica wondered whether he might feel apprehensive about meeting her parents. He was sensitive; it was one of the things she liked about him, along with his original way of looking at things and his kindness towards her and his eyes, which irresistibly drew hers.

'We could go for a walk after dinner if it's not completely dark. Maybe down to the pub in the village if my parents don't mind us going out again straight away.'

She pictured the small low-ceilinged pub with its huge stone fireplace and few dining tables. Those standing at the bar would turn to stare as she and Chris came through the door; they would look Chris up and down and make good-humoured wisecracks. But once the jokes were over, they could sit in the corner and talk freely. It might be easier than sitting in the living room at home with her mother, at least for the first evening.

She had never brought a boyfriend home before. She had talked about Chris on the phone of course and knew that her parents wanted to meet him. She had asked her mother as nonchalantly as she could whether they could come home for the weekend and had heard the intake of breath before the swift agreement. She might find it difficult to meet her mother's eyes this evening. But once the first awkwardness was over, they would have the whole weekend together and she would show him the milking parlour and the calves and her favourite place by the river, and they could drive to the coast to walk on the beach and everything that was familiar would be intensified by his presence and her closeness to him.

At Yeoford a woman got on with a golden retriever wearing a bright red collar. She settled into a seat and smiled around at the other passengers, the dog seeming to smile too and almost everyone on the carriage responding and talking, warmed by the promise in the May sunshine.

'It isn't always like this,' Jessica said, 'Sometimes it's really crowded and people have to stand and there's a lot of complaining, but mostly people are quite sympathetic to each other.'

'It's way different from trains around London. Nobody speaks there.' He pulled a face to show how aloof people could be and Jessica laughed at him.

'I wanted to get away from Devon at one time, before I went to university. I thought people – not my parents, but others – were complacent, self-satisfied, like the cows over there chewing the cud. Like they didn't know about the real world out there. But now I love coming back.'

'You don't mind me coming too?' Doubt flashed through his eyes and she kissed him, unable to express in any other way just how much she didn't mind.

The train rocked past the little stone-built gabled houses built for station masters, Copplestone, Morchard Bishop, Lapford, now unattended but still neat and expectant in the late afternoon sun, decorated with hanging baskets and tubs of flowers. At Eggesford it slowed and stopped. Two Painted Lady butterflies chased and danced together above the flowers before coming to rest one above the other, joined as one, their wings flicking gently.

In the next row of seats, a boy of four or five played with his baby sister who sat on her father's lap. He hid his face behind his hands then jumped out with a loud 'Boo!' and his sister laughed helplessly, reaching out her hands like little starfish to encourage him to repeat the trick. The two were enthralled by each other and the parents watched in delight and exchanged eloquent looks, all four sharing a love that was as pure and bright as a spring flower. Jessica watched, fascinated. What circumstances had brought the parents together? How many years of sharing had produced those two children? She saw that Chris was watching too and she turned away, bewilderingly self-conscious. From the window she saw the wayside trees opening, budding and flowering with irresistible vitality and she felt herself to be in love with Devon and in love with Chris.

'What's the matter?' He was looking at her, amused, and she realised that her eyes had widened in surprise at her thoughts.

'Nothing.' She squeezed his hand and he interlaced his fingers with hers. She hadn't voiced that thought to herself before. She tried the phrase out again in her head. I love him. It was true, surely.

'What are you smiling at now? Tell me!' He was sitting sideways in his seat so he could see her properly, his eyes alive with amusement.

'Just that I absolutely know you'll like Devon!' She brushed her lips against his cheek and they kissed until she gently drew back, aware that the woman sitting across the aisle was smiling at them. She rested her hand on his leg, her palm acutely aware of the taut thigh muscle beneath the cotton fabric.

Chris stroked her knee.

'Is it much further to Barnstaple?'

'No, we're nearly there.'

The line crossed and re-crossed the Taw, the river widening and growing in strength, certain of its course through water meadows bright with yellow iris, soon to run beneath Barnstaple's ancient many-arched bridge and widen still further until it joined with its partner, the Torridge, and became one with the sea. Soon the train would slow and run gently into Barnstaple station and she would see her mother, a little flustered, waiting expectantly on the platform.

'Look, we're nearly there!' And they rose hand in hand, with the weekend and the whole summer and perhaps the years stretching gloriously in front of them.

On the Beach

Leah was woken by shrill crying. She turned and pulled the duvet over her head to shut out the noise and the sunlight that streamed in through the thin curtain, but after a few minutes Kyra was crying even more loudly. Leah crawled out, intending to bring her daughter into bed with her but she was standing up in her cot in the corner of the room with tear-filled eyes, a downturned mouth and an obviously dirty nappy.

'Come on then, you mucky little toad.'

She kissed her daughter and carried her into the bathroom, moving aside the old baby bath which was placed in the centre of the floor to catch drips from the skylight. Twice she had summoned up enough courage to go into the letting agent's and ask them to get the skylight fixed, but nothing had been done. The bath was almost half full so the rain must have been heavy again overnight. It was typical of this summer, nothing but oppressive grey skies and rain day after day; it was said to be the wettest June on record and it must be true because she had hardly left the flat all month. But there was no pitter-patter of rain on the skylight this morning, only the footsteps of the seagull that was nesting up there. She looked up and saw the broad webbed feet of the gull strutting across the Perspex, then a fierce yellow beak pecking at its edges as if it would find a way in. Disgusting thing. She yelled at it to clear off and the gull raised its wings and shrieked aggressively.

She changed and dressed Kyra, holding her on her lap while combing her wispy blond hair into ponytails high on her head and fastening them with pink ribbons.

'Who's pretty then? Who's a pretty little maid?'

She held her daughter high above her head and shook her gently until she laughed her deep, gurgling laugh that made the problems with leaking roofs and hostile gulls seem less pressing. She put her on the lounge floor with a biscuit to eat, turned on the television, and went to find herself a T-shirt to pull over her pyjamas. The sun illuminated the untidy bed and piles of clothes on the chair, but she couldn't make it look any better because the clothes developed mould in the cupboard. She pushed up the sash window. The room caught the sun for about an hour, just between the time it rose above the roofs opposite and disappeared behind her own, if it shone at all, which was rare these days.

She could see down to the High Street from here. When she was pregnant and Jamie was with her, they would sit together on the window seat with the window pushed wide open and the music up loud; they could shout out if they saw friends on the High Street and throw down the key for them. Sometimes there were eight or ten up here; Jamie would sit with his arm around her and they had some great times.

She had thought that she and Jamie and Kyra would be a proper family, but after a few boastful weeks he started to resent the amount of attention Kyra needed. Leah tried her best but always seemed to say or do the wrong thing and make him angry, and he started staying out more frequently and sometimes not coming home at night although she waited up for him. When he finally moved out, he took the CD player with him, so of course none of that crowd came up anymore.

He still came back from time to time; she wasn't always sure whether it was her or Kyra he wanted to see. Sometimes it was her, but she always managed to upset him again and he would get angry and walk out. It hurt just as much, every time. He was with Sherie now anyway; she had seen them from the window, fooling around and kissing as they walked down the High Street.

She sat on the window seat and wrapped her arms around her knees. From here she could watch people without them ever noticing her. She could see several people walking purposefully down the hill to work and a grey-looking man on a mobility scooter waiting outside the betting shop. Then along came the woman who wore a man's hat and let her dog crap on the pavement every morning, and the dustcart grinding its way up the steep hill. Bideford's streets were very hilly and sometimes she wished she lived somewhere else, especially with the buggy to push. But it was where she grew up and she knew she would never move. Some people did. Some of the kids who stayed on at school moved away to go to university.

Her life wouldn't be too bad if she could find a better flat. Every now and then she enquired about social housing, usually when the damp was particularly bad and was making Kyra's asthma worse, but she was always told that her name was a long way down the list. She had heard that housing benefit was going to be stopped for people under 25. If that was true she would be evicted and she didn't know what she would do. Where would she go? She couldn't go to her mum's because she was never going to live in the same house as Jason. There was no way she would trust him with Kyra. She had never understood what her mum saw in him. Sometimes she woke sweating and afraid in the night, having dreamt that she and Kyra had nowhere to sleep and were sitting on a bench in the park with their clothes in carrier bags.

The sun was almost warm on her face. Sitting here, she noticed the angles and colours of the roofs and the crooked chimneys and the blue sky above that. Where the wall and roof met on the dilapidated building across the road, there were cracks where flowers grew, the leaves and magenta flowers brilliant in the sunshine. She leant further out of the window and twisted round to look up towards her own roof and the same flowers were growing there, their roots pushing deep into the wall and finding sustenance where there appeared to be none.

There was a whirr of wheels and a boy on a skateboard shot down the middle of the High Street, his knees bent and his body poised as if he would launch himself into the air and join the seagulls that wheeled above the rooftops. How was it that he had the nerve to skim along against the flow of the traffic when she found it difficult to summon enough energy to walk to the shop? She spent most of her time on the sofa with Kyra watching television. She really should get out. She could take Kyra down to the park, meet up with Katie and her kids. Or even go to the beach. Why not? It was a sunny day; other people went to the beach.

When Leah was young and her parents were still together, when the thought of her mother ever walking out was unimaginable, they used to have caravan holidays in Cornwall and spend every day on the beach. The summers were as they should be, instead of rain all the time. She and her brother had buckets and spades and an inflatable ball decorated in brightly coloured segments. She remembered the sensation of the soft sand under her bare feet and the strength of her father's hands as he helped her jump high over the waves, and walking into the town with feet still bare, to buy fish and chips and ice cream. In the afternoons her mother would sit in a folding chair reading magazines, while her father helped Leah and her brother to build a boat out of sand to sit in when the tide drew near, safe for a while as they sat side by side watching the water swirling all around them, until finally the first wave broke over the prow.

Kyra had never been to the beach. She had never walked barefoot on the sand or paddled in the sea. She spent all her days cooped up in a tiny damp flat, instead of having the freedom of a beach that stretches as far as the eye can see. Katie took her kids to the beach sometimes – they could go together. Usually Katie was the organiser, the one who persuaded Leah to go to the Children's Centre and advised her on losing weight, who was hoping to go to college one day a week so that she could get a job when her children were old enough. But this time Leah would be making the suggestions. She reached for her phone.

Two hours later she stood at the bus stop on the Quay waiting for Katie. It wasn't boring to stand and wait because there were so many things to look at: the river with its tree-lined banks and the boats moored alongside, the traffic passing on the Quay and all the people walking past the bus stop. She saw some people she knew and there were tourists about too - it was easy to recognise them because they wore shorts and waterproofs and wandered along with expressions of vacant contentment. A big ship was being loaded with timber and, further along, some men were pulling ropes and chains from a fishing boat and laying them out along the quayside in order of length. She shouted across the road to her cousin from East-the-Water, telling him she was off to the beach.

'Don't get wet then!' he yelled back, which was a strange thing to say, because of course she would get wet when they paddled.

Kyra gazed up at her sleepily and Leah crouched down and straightened the ribbons in her hair.

'Who's going to the beach, then? Who's a lucky girl today?'

She rocked the buggy gently until Kyra's eyes closed. An elderly woman in the bus queue smiled and asked whether she was a good sleeper, and whether she was beginning to talk yet; Leah answered all her questions and told her how Kyra was going to love paddling in the sea and being swung over the little waves streaming in over the sand. It was the best thing in the world sometimes, being a mother.

She counted her money again. There should be enough for the bus fare and some fish and chips and perhaps an ice cream. She had to keep two or three pounds for tomorrow's food, but there should be enough in the electricity meter until her next cash came through.

A bus arrived and left. Katie was late. Leah leaned against the bus shelter half-listening to all the talk going on around her. After another five minutes her phone rang.

Katie couldn't come. Her cousin had been arrested for drugs – 'Again! The idiot!' she said, and she had to help her aunt because she was so upset.

Leah stared out along the Quay. There was no one else who would go to the beach with her. Marie had no money. Her mother was always either working at the care home or asleep. Her father would have come if he could but was away working, delivering in the north of England. When the next bus came in, she didn't hesitate; she would go alone.

When she got off the bus, there was the sea; a vast expanse of sapphire stretching out to meet the sky, so bright and jewel-like that she stopped in surprise, causing an elderly man to bump into her. She used to come to Westward Ho! three or four years ago when she was about fifteen but she couldn't remember really noticing the sea, probably because she was too busy chatting with the boys who gathered at the sea wall. She walked down there now and leant on the wall along with the tourists who were eating dripping ice cream cones and gazing out at the silvery glint of the beach and the long lines of surf. Above the low hiss of the waves were the musical voices of children; she looked beyond the ridge of blue-grey pebbles and saw children with nets balanced gingerly on the rocks above glassy pools, and she remembered the sharp rocks under her feet and the silkiness of underwater seaweed in her hands, like newly washed hair.

Kyra was waking and beginning to whine so Leah unstrapped her and lifted her up to sit on the lichen-covered wall.

'Seaside, Kyra! We're at the seaside!'

She nuzzled the child's plump little neck, inhaling the scent of baby lotion along with that of salt and seaweed snatched from the beach by a brisk wind. Kyra laughed and tried to grab Leah's nose.

'Look at the waves, Kyra!'

She pointed to the beach where the waves ran in across a mile or more of level sand, further than the eye could see. Kyra grabbed her finger then wriggled around to hold on to

Leah's hair so she could pull herself up to stand on the wall. She bounced up and down against her mother's restraining hands, shouting 'Down! Down!' Leah lifted her down and held her hand as she walked unsteadily along the pavement, but she was fretful and difficult, wanting to sit down or to walk in the road. It would be best to have lunch before they went any further.

She strapped Kyra back in her buggy, put the dummy in her mouth and crossed the road to the fish and chip shop. There was a display of brightly-coloured beach toys outside an adjoining shop; she looked at the price list in the window of the fish and chip shop and then walked over to the buckets and spades. She could not afford both. She chose a purple bucket with a smiling orange fish on the side for £1.50 and a small spade for £1, and then bought a portion of chips.

Behind an expanse of yellow paving was a semi-circle of benches where people sat as if waiting for a performance. Leah sat alongside an elderly couple and shared her chips with Kyra. It would have been more fun if Katie and her children had come too; there was no one she recognised among the families and groups of friends.

'Aren't you cold, love?' The woman sitting on the bench had just pulled on a cardigan because the strong breeze blowing from the sea had become quite chilly.

'I am a bit. It was much warmer in Bideford.'

'You should try and keep the little one warm.'

She was wearing shorts and a vest and Kyra was in a sundress; it had not occurred to her to bring anything warmer. It was summer, after all.

'She'll be all right; she'll keep warm running around on the beach.'

But she felt rather foolish and got up and walked away as soon as she could.

On the green there was a slide in the shape of a boat that Kyra would have enjoyed but the older children playing on it were pushing one another other from the top and shouting aggressively at one another. She looked up at the luxury flats that formed a long curve along the seafront. The windows faced right out to sea and had private glass-fronted balconies containing comfortable reclining chairs and one had a glass table with two goblets of wine just waiting for someone to come and drink them; you could almost imagine it would be someone famous. Fancy having that view from your front room! But it was too cold to stand and watch because the flats cast a deep shadow, blocking the sun from the public walkway, and Kyra was beginning to whimper and pull at her harness.

'You can't come out now! Soon, on the beach.'

Beyond the block of apartments, a row of beach huts in pastel colours lined up behind a white picket fence. Couples in deckchairs sat on the little lawns of two or three huts but most were tightly shuttered. The wind was stronger here so she turned back.

To her right, the houses and flats which formed the village gleamed in the sun against the dark backdrop of a steep wooded hill. If Katie had been with her, they would probably have gone into the village to look at the shops, but as she had no money to spend she continued along the seafront and carefully bumped the buggy down the steps. Her shoes were too tight and she could feel a blister beginning to develop; it would be a relief to take them off on the sand.

At the top of the slipway was a hut where you could hire surfboards and deckchairs or buy colourful toys. Shiny purple and gold windmills caught the light and spun noisily in the breeze and Leah wheeled Kyra over to see them.

'Look, Kyra, windmills!' She only meant Kyra to admire them but she stretched out her hands and started to cry loudly. The windmills cost £2. Leah turned quickly away.

'You can't have anything you want, Kyra!' She meant to say 'everything you want' but didn't bother to correct herself.

Down on the sand a group of ten or twelve barefoot young people were talking in loud, confident voices. She heard snatches of conversation about wind and surf, and laughter at mystifying jokes. The girls were lithe and beautiful with long sun-bleached hair and the boys had tanned, muscular arms, and they all wore skin-tight wetsuits or knee-length shorts slung low on the hips. Several held surf boards under their arms and some were playing Frisbee. The blue Frisbee glided from one to another as if it had a life and a purpose of its own, flying so low that it almost skimmed the sand or sailing high against the sky and turning apparently of its own volition, as if attracted irresistibly back to the group. The surfers caught it and guided it back on its way without interrupting their conversation, even those who carried long surf boards stretching over to catch it with perfect balance. With a flick of the wrist it was sent spinning behind two people and up into the hand of another, then away again, high over all their heads to hang almost motionless before turning and floating down to be caught again. Leah watched, fascinated by the group's supple movements and their effortless ability to catch the spinning blue disc. A tall boy with dark shoulder length hair sent it on its way then put his arm around one of the girls and caressed her, and she ran her fingers through her wind-tangled hair and reclined against him, an image of perfect relaxation against the huge backdrop of golden sand and sky.

Leah went down the slipway with the buggy. At the bottom there was a steep step and a deep pool of water, so she had to put the brakes on, jump across the water and then lift the buggy across; it was heavy and awkward and she almost lost her balance, only saving herself by putting her foot in the pool, whereupon her shoe filled with water. Embarrassed, she was quickly pushing Kyra across the sand past the group of young people when suddenly the Frisbee shot past the intertwined couple and hit the side of the buggy with a loud clatter. Kyra started to cry and Leah screamed at the boy who threw it.

'What the *fuck* do you think you're doing? Fucking idiot!'

He hurried over and picked up the Frisbee, lifeless now on the sand.

'I'm really sorry. I didn't mean to hurt her. She's ok, isn't she?'

'You could have fucking killed her!'

She stalked off across the beach, shaking with rage, but heard the comments from one of the girls, and then a boy.

'Now, now, let's not lose our temper.'

'Did you ever see such a fat arse, anyway?'

There was a flurry of laughter and she sensed their eyes on her as she pushed the buggy away as fast as she could. She felt her shorts riding up her bottom but didn't dare pull them down for fear of further laughter. Her heel was stinging and her shoes were pinching her feet but she didn't want to stop to take them off while they could still see her, and as the pain increased, so did her anger. Finally she could stand the pain in her heel no longer and she stopped and looked back. They had gone. The beach was empty. She sat on the wet sand and took off her shoes. Her heel was rubbed raw. She was close to tears.

The surfers had been on the best part of the beach. From the slipway she had seen groups of people in the distance but the beach was almost deserted now. The last family was crossing the pebble ridge, a man and woman carrying two young children balanced precariously as they stepped from one big round pebble to another. Much further on, a solitary man with a metal detector searched the ridge. The tide was a very long way out, leaving a huge expanse of brown wet sand; it was just her and Kyra, with no one near.

'Come on Kyra, come out on the sand.'

She unstrapped her from the buggy and took off her shoes.

'Feel the sand under your feet!'

Kyra whined and squatted down, trying to brush off the wet sand. Leah looked around for somewhere to sit and moved towards some large pebbles with pools of water around them at the foot of the ridge. Perhaps the salt water would ease the pain in her heel. Kyra toddled after her and sat down in the puddle.

'Not there, Kyra!'

She took away a piece of seaweed that Kyra was about to put in her mouth and threw it up on to the pebble ridge. She had imagined that there would be sun and people with picnics and other children for Kyra to play with, but the wind was sending ever greyer clouds scudding across the sky.

'Come on Kyra, let's build a sandcastle.'

She tried to show her how to fill the bucket, but the spade was barely strong enough for the wet, tightly packed sand and when she gave it to Kyra, she dropped it and went back to sit in the puddle. Leah turned the bucket over. The wet sand collapsed drunkenly into an untidy pile and a second effort produced the same result. There were no pretty shells for decoration. She had pictured a perfectly square castle with ramparts and turrets and a moat into which the waves would swirl when the tide came in. Even if she could have built the castle, the tide was much too far out and it would be hours before it reached the pebble ridge again. She stood up and gazed out across the flat expanse of brown sand, hearing the roar of the distant surf and the jeering calls of gulls, silvery white specks perched on the shoreline. The clouds shifted and a sharp band of sunlight glinted angrily on to the white-topped waves, then disappeared behind the thick grey cloud again. Perhaps if she walked down to the water's edge, she could make a boat carved out of sand the way her father used to. And Kyra could paddle. It was a waste to come all this way and not go in the sea. She shivered at the emptiness of the endless sand and sea and the huge sky. She lifted Kyra out of the water and strapped her into the buggy, ignoring her angry roar, and headed out across the empty sands.

She walked and she walked and Kyra didn't stop crying. The ripples of sand were hard under her bare feet and when she crossed a wetter area, it pulled at her as if it would suck her in. The wind whipped her hair back from her face and stung her ears and made her eyes and nose run; it was a fight to walk against its strength and when she paused to turn her back to it and regain her breath, she saw the tracks that the buggy has made, wavering in tentative lines from the pebble ridge although she thought she had kept a straight course.

There was a low threatening mutter and she looked up to see the outstretched wings and yellow claws of a gull against a gunmetal sky and she ducked and screamed, but when she looked up again the sky was empty and she saw the gull land with others at the water's edge, strutting and eyeing her suspiciously. As she approached the line of surf, the hiss of the wheels on the wet sand was drowned by the roar of a wave rushing to meet her and she had to shout to make herself heard.

'Look at the sea, Kyra!'

She was unsure whether she should continue on or run from the advancing tide. Hesitating by the line of dirty foam and stranded seaweed, she felt spray on her face that seemed to come from the surf smashing on to the beach, until she looked up and saw a spreading mass of black cloud. At once the rain reached them and she snatched Kyra from her buggy and held her close to her chest, turning from the wind to shield the little pink-ribboned head from the deluge that came in horizontal sheets, and her cries joined with the sea's roar of protest.

Despite her attempts to protect Kyra, the rain was streaming from their hair and stinging their bare shoulders; she stumbled with her head down, away from the fast-moving tide that washed away everything that was safe and familiar, holding Kyra against her and dragging the buggy behind her. Kyra's little legs felt cold and wet and she clung to Leah crying,

'Mummy, mummy, mummy!'

'All right, sweetheart, it's all right. I'll soon get you dry and warm again.'

She tried to sound confident but she remembered that she had not replaced the old bath under the skylight, so the rain would be coming in, soaking the carpet and perhaps running through to the flat below. She looked up and, through the grey mist that had almost obscured the village, she made out the distant bulk of the apartment block above the shoreline and saw, here and there, a glow of warm light from the windows.

Surely someone there would help her. And she pictured the huge warm rooms with comfortable sofas and glass tables and the windows, the big windows that looked right out on to the beach. Someone would see her. Surely someone would notice her and would care.

The Journey

He has been walking for nineteen days; the record he writes in the road atlas tells him so. Last night he wrote, 'Day 19, Minehead to Porlock.' It was late June when he left Birmingham so it must be well into July now.

He closes the atlas on his lap and from his vantage point stares out at the vast, silent sea bounded only by the hazy outline of Wales on the horizon. It is the first time on his journey that he has been able to look at his surroundings without the fear of being observed. Below and to his right is the bay around which he walked yesterday, Porlock Bay; a gentle indentation in the coastline protected to the east by a cradling arm with an undulating breast of hills above; a perfect composition in emerald and sapphire such as he has seen in books. The measured white-tipped waves, running in towards the shingle ridge, gasp softly as they expire on the beach, a sound that calmed him on his arrival and throughout the night. He turns, pushing his hood back from his face, to see the oak woodland stretching up behind him to a horizon already made indistinct by a heat haze. There will be walkers soon, but he is well back from the path. He and his tent will be obscured by the bracken.

He started seeing walkers when he left Minehead. There were walkers the last time he was here with his parents and sister nearly thirty years ago, but there are more of them now, more of everything in England now. Cars. Houses. Now the walkers wear bright colours and thick-soled boots and some of them use two walking sticks, despite seeming fit and healthy. They pass within touching distance so he'll keep off the footpaths, during the day at least.

It's a diversion, coming across Exmoor. The flower book gave him the idea. He saw it in the window of a second-hand bookshop in Birmingham and went back during the day to

69

buy it. *The Observer's Book of Wild Flowers*. He and his sister Carol had a copy of the same book when they were children, and *Observer's Books* on wild animals and birds. They had *I Spy* books too. He remembered them when he saw the book in the shop window and they reminded him of the family holidays on Exmoor, the open moors and the brown ponies, the coldness of the water and the feel of the rounded stones under his feet when he paddled in the streams.

The book has a pale green cover and the spine is faded to a light brown. It fits comfortably in his hand and he likes the feel of the pages made fine and soft through use. Tessa, his support worker, never saw the book because he kept it under his bed until he was ready to leave, along with the tent he bought from an army surplus store and the road atlas he found in the recycling bin. If she'd known about his plans she might have tried to stop him, thinking he would get into difficulties, and now she will never know because he's not going back even though he would like her to know what he has done. 'You planned something for yourself and you followed it through, it's a great achievement!' that's what she would have said.

He had been thinking for several years about seeing his sister again, and when he finally started on independent living again, he began to plan. He worked out that the walk to Okehampton with the diversion across Exmoor should take three or four weeks. The timing is about right so far, but it doesn't matter if he's late as she's not expecting him. He takes the address book from his inside pocket and leafs through the worn pages to stare again at the address in Okehampton. It's nearly twenty years since he heard from her.

He set off with great optimism but the roads from Birmingham were busy; as each car passed he had to brace himself for the onrush of the next because they came so quickly. Sometimes the cars slowed so that the occupants could look at him and several times something was shouted. He could feel his anxiety rising and concentrated on counting to shut out the cars and the people. He counted a hundred paces, then another, then another. In his head the uneven numbers were high notes and the even ones low, creating a rhythm like a clock ticking while he walked. He decided to try walking at night because that was what he used to do in Birmingham, but it wasn't safe to sleep out in the daytime. In Gloucester he had been woken by a kick in the small of his back and there was a gang of kids surrounding him, jeering and laughing. So he slept at night, behind hedges and once behind a motorway embankment where the traffic growled but never found him. Once, in a field, he slept late in the morning and woke, sunshine streaming through the thin material of the tent, to hear a roaring which turned into a human voice. When it did not go away he crawled out and there were boots and he glimpsed a thick-set man with a red face, his voice gravelly and very loud. He pulled out the tent pegs as fast as he could and bundled up the tent, dropping his atlas and only just managing to pick it up again. The voice ceased but he knew the man still stood there, his hands on his hips, staring. He stumbled off, almost slipping as he climbed over the gate, and it was a long time before he dared to look back. He remembered what his doctor had said and he took extra medication.

But when he was past Minehead, he could walk for several minutes before a car passed. He started to notice the sky and the drifting clouds that dissipated as the sun grew hotter. As he strode past the hedges, he noticed the flowers, and when he stopped he found their long-forgotten names in the *Observer's Book*. He wanted to record the prevalence of each species, so he worked out a system. After every hundred paces he pauses to mark with a small pencilled line all the flowers he has seen and after he has made four lines, he strikes a line through them for the fifth sighting. It works well and it keeps his mind busy, which is good because he has been missing his studying. He has been studying a book called *Inheritance and Natural History*. Tessa used to say, 'It's good to have something to concentrate on, but wouldn't you like a change?'

She didn't understand that there was still a lot in the book that he had to learn. He used to read some of the early pages to Tessa when she asked him about it; the first pages were the easiest because they explained what the book was about - the differences that exist between individuals in a population and the mechanism for transmitting characteristics from one generation to another. As the book went on, it got harder. He would begin to understand it, at least in relation to flowers which were more straightforward than people, but then his understanding would get hazy and disappear, as if someone had removed it from his mind. Tessa said, 'Try to tell me *why* it interests you.' When he didn't answer she said, 'Why don't you try a novel instead?'

The sea is huge and calming; today he must turn his back on it and begin to cross the moor, but that too will be open and empty. He packs up the tent, swings his bag on to his back and starts to walk. The trees shut out all but a small ribbon of sky and the pattern on the lane is of bright sunlight and deep shadow. There are birds singing deep in the woodland and a repetitive high-pitched cry he remembers to be a young buzzard calling for food; there may be deer and foxes, badgers too. He could go into the forest and never see another person, live a secluded, secret existence. But he wants to find his sister.

The track follows the contour of a steep hillside; luxuriant bracken and meadowsweet lean in towards him. After a hundred paces he marks foxglove, rosebay willowherb, meadowsweet and tormentil. When he reaches the top of the hill a wide view opens out unexpectedly; bright green pasture dropping away into a deep valley then rising again to the muted mauve and dun moorland, an austere and empty expanse over which he runs his eyes to plan his route.

By mid-afternoon he is counting his paces on a narrow lane which meanders through the valley. His feet are aching and he feels his strength diminishing, so he climbs through a barbed wire fence into a wood and sleeps for a while, lulled by the murmuring of a wood pigeon. Then he walks on until the light begins to fade and he climbs over a gate into a field where, hidden from the lane by the high hedge, he eats half a loaf and some cheese, tearing at the bread in his hunger. Two fields away and just visible through a gap in the hedge, four or five large brightly-coloured tents are spread out alongside the river, several with a camp fire glowing alongside. A Land Rover drives into the far side of the camping ground and stops at each tent in turn. The campers, who are gathered companionably around their little fires, turn to the visitor and pass him money, their cheerful voices and their laughter drifting across the fields. When the Land Rover leaves, a man stands and shouts towards the tree-lined river. 'Ben! Ellie! Time for bed!' And two children clamber up the bank and chase each other towards the tent.

The distant voices and laughter break into the silence around him. Sitting with his legs crossed, he closes his eyes and he is sixteen again, hunched uncomfortably on the damp ground around a fire, a reluctant participant on a school camping trip. The ribald jokes and roars of raucous teenage laughter from the other boys alternated with long silences during which he listened to the crackle of the flames, stared into the embers which glowed and dimmed, and felt the heat of his face.

An hour passes and the wind rises and clouds race threateningly across the darkening sky; the sides of the valley turn black, seeming to grow taller and close in on him. He hastily puts up the tent and lies listening to the voices from the campsite, to the bleating of sheep and a distant fox barking, trying to shut out the imagined dark hills that rise ever higher and nearer until they press against him. He sleeps fitfully, cold despite his layers of clothes, and disturbed by dreams and heavy squalls of rain that beat against the thin sides of the tent.

In the morning he rises quickly, standing on the wet grass to eat some bread. He packs away his tent and checks the lane in both directions before climbing over the gate. Some campers are already moving about and the smell of bacon drifts over the fields. The green valley walls are gently rounded under an azure sky scattered with soft white cloud, as if he has woken in a different place, and he strides over puddles drying in the sun. There is a sign by the side of the road. *Brendon Show. A day out for all the family. Sunday 14th August,* and almost at once there are cottages, then a village green with a seat and signpost and a tree, like the picture on a biscuit tin that his mother used to have. He had not meant to sleep so near a village. He pulls his hood further forward and walks steadily on, eyes on the road, glimpsing a man watching from a garden; 'Maggie!' the man calls, 'quick, Maggie!', then there is again just the tarmac, the hedges with flowers and the sound of a river rushing over stones; the man is not following him.

He turns into a gateway and studies the map. He is a little further on than he had realised and should have no difficulty reaching Simonsbath this evening. The open moor is too exposed for pitching his tent; near the village there should be hedges to shelter him. Perhaps also a shop; he had not been prepared and did not look carefully enough in Brendon. The remaining bread and cheese should be sufficient for today but that is all.

He walks on; the lane leaves the river and winds up a hill between high banks and he marks foxglove, common toadflax and field scabious. The climb makes him hot and he takes off his parka and stuffs it into his bag, pulling up the hood of his sweatshirt instead. Around a bend there is a sudden commotion and movement and he stops, heart pounding. A sheep and two well-grown lambs dart from the hedge where they have been grazing and turn to stare at him, wild-eyed. They are sheep, that is all; it was only the sudden movement that startled him. He can see now that they are uneasy at his unexpected appearance; as soon as he takes a step forward they turn and run up the road, cumbersome bodies on stick legs, but they turn and hesitate, wanting to go back the way they came. He stands very still; hesitantly, in fits and starts, they retrace their steps, keeping close to the opposite hedge then dashing past him, the mother first and the skittish lambs close behind. He watches them disappear around the corner, having resolved a difficulty he had never even encountered before.

After a quarter of a mile or so the hedges disappear like a horse's blinkers being removed and he crosses a cattle grid on to the moor. The view before him is a wide, billowing expanse of muted browns and mauves interspersed with yellow gorse from which the warmth of the sun coaxes a sweet scent. He lengthens his stride and looks up as he walks, his gaze reaching to the far horizon, and he sees there are no dangers ahead, no hidden places to harbour surprises and when a car approaches and passes him, he averts his eyes and maintains a steady pace. There are occasional pull-ins containing parked cars; next to one, a man and a woman are sitting in canvas chairs. In a quick glance he sees that the man is reading the *Mirror*, and the woman has her face turned to the sun and her eyes closed. The man says, 'Jean, look; look at that.' As he walks on, he imagines all the other things that are being said, but he remembers Tessa's advice and breathes to calm himself.

The tall spikes of rosebay willowherb line his route, magenta flowers at their tips and fluffy seedheads below, which at the slightest breeze drift from the mother plant and catch in his beard and long hair. A long-forgotten image comes to him and he stops suddenly to look; his parents are sitting on the picnic rug, there. They are younger than he is now; his mother with her full skirt and permed hair pouring tea from a tartan-patterned flask, his father relaxed without his tie; he and Carol are running after the ethereal air-borne seeds and jumping to catch them, their mother shouting to them, 'Be careful! Mind the picnic!' He was older and could jump higher. 'I've got lots, look!' he called to Carol, and he opened his fist to show her, but his hand was empty.

Carol was better at remembering the names of flowers than he was, but when he tried to teach her about the life cycle of newts or the difference between frogs and toads, she listened, her face upturned to his, and then always forgot what he told her. But she liked flowers. And she had a flower press - of course! The sudden memory makes him stop again in the road. Two blocks of wood with wing nuts to screw them together - and her album with the faded blooms carefully arranged with little strips of yellowing Sellotape to hold them in place and the spellings he helped her with in her childish handwriting underneath. Might she still have the album? He has an idea; he will pick one example of every plant he sees and press it between the pages of the *Observer's Book* and give it to her when he reaches Okehampton. When he pictures her smiling, he sees her as a child. She didn't smile when she last visited him in hospital; she would have been in her early twenties then and she hadn't visited since she came with their parents several years before, the last time he ever saw them. She must be over forty now, but she surely won't have changed very much. He stoops to see the purple heather and golden gorse, intermingled as if flowers of different species could grow from the same root. He carefully picks the best examples and places them between the pages of the book. The description for gorse states that 'one may gather enormous trusses of deliciously fragrant flowers - if one is not deterred by its formidable spikes.' As he walks on, he repeats the words so that he can remember them and tell Carol.

The next stretch of moorland has been burnt, a charred hillside stretching up from the road. He crouches to examine the black, twisted stems of gorse and sees that fresh green shoots are already growing from the base; the slope that looks black and dead will, in a year or so, be cloaked in fragrant yellow flowers again, a colourful future growing from a dark past. For an hour or more there is just the steady rhythm of his boots as he walks and walks, the sun on his face and the wind in his hair, his only companions the rippling grass of the moor and the passing clouds in the expansive sky.

Gradually the road across the moor winds down to Simonsbath and hedges again obscure his view. It is late afternoon when he reaches the village. The houses are large and stand in their own grounds; there is a hotel and a shop called the Farmer's Den. There is no food in the window, just boots and coats, ropes, tarpaulins and fishing gear. A woman stares out at him and he walks quickly on, past the hotel where people are eating at outside tables and out of the village again on a road lined with beech hedges. They protect him when, after a half a mile or so, he climbs over a gate to rest up for the night. He finishes the last of the bread and cheese, trying not to think about setting off in the morning without breakfast.

He is walking by eight, having judged from the road atlas that it is about five miles to Exford. It is out of his way but there will surely be a shop; his stomach is already aching with hunger. By nine thirty he reaches the village sign; a woman is putting out umbrellas in the garden of a big pub; there are thatched cottages and a large green and, on the far side, two or three shops. A man in a short-sleeved shirt stands outside a shop, watching him as he approaches and opens the door. A bell rings and the hum of voices ceases. He finds a basket and picks up three loaves, some sardines, cheese, two packets of biscuits and then he hears Tessa's voice, 'You must remember to buy fruit and veg. You need to keep healthy.' So he picks out two oranges and two apples even though the prices are high. On the counter there are Cornish pasties in an oven with glass sides and the gnawing in his stomach is even stronger than his desire to be out of the shop. He points, and a woman puts one in a bag. As he closes the door, the people start talking again.

'Well, did you ever...?'

'Quick, where's the air freshener?'

A seat on the green faces away from the shops and he sits down and devours the pasty, swallowing the peppery meat and potato almost without chewing, then picking the flakes of pastry from his parka and eating those too.

'Must be the same chap as George saw up near Brendon,' says a voice.

As the warm food soothes him, he thinks about the things that have been said. He used to imagine that people knew his thoughts and were talking about him when they were not, but this time the words *are* about him. He had always resisted Tessa's efforts to make him less conspicuous. When he reaches Carol's house, she will understand and will be able to help him.

He packs the food into his bag and walks away without looking back, setting a steady pace back up the road. It was the voices that kept him in hospital for so long. Several times he came out but the voices drove him back in again. Sometimes he heard them plotting when he was alone. He can keep them away almost all the time, even now when something is shouted from one of the cars that are accelerating past him.

A gateway gives a sudden view of a green pasture and half a dozen black-faced sheep scurry away in alarm, then turn to stare at him before re-joining the rest of the flock. But there is one… it is lying motionless away from the others, dead, he is sure, then suddenly struggling wildly, its thin legs sticking up from the massive bulk of its body. It is motionless again and surely not breathing now, until the panic-stricken fight begins again. He walks away up the road as fast as he can, but then turns and runs back and climbs the gate. He approaches the sheep and its eyes roll in terror at him as it struggles helplessly again and he takes handfuls of the rank wool and heaves at the dead weight and suddenly it is up and running and he climbs back over the gate, his heart pounding and his hands shaking. The sheep is grazing with the others as if nothing has happened, and he is the one who rescued it.

He once found an injured blackbird in the garden at home, chattering with fear as it struggled to escape his approach, hopping and falling helplessly on its damaged leg. He would have been about ten, old enough to feel ashamed afterwards that he had run into the house screaming for help and that it was Carol, speaking softly, who cornered the bird and placed it gently in a box with a lid so that the darkness would calm it.

Together they carried it to the man down the road who had a way with birds.

He will tell her about the sheep, that he helped it, saved its life perhaps.

Striding along the grey ribbon of tarmac that cuts across the high open moor, he can surely see the curvature of the earth, so far-reaching is the view. From the heather and gorse at his feet, the bare sweep of moorland runs on and on until it meets the sky that arcs over him; he pauses to gaze up at the fast-moving clouds, the sun and wind in his face, then turns slowly to take in the emptiness that stretches in every direction. There is a continuous rich outpouring of birdsong, a pure, high-pitched sound that he associates with open air and freedom, and he squints until he sees a small brown bird high above that is rising with flickering wings, plunging down and rising steadily again. A few hundred metres away a small herd of Exmoor ponies and their foals are grazing amongst the tussocky grass and heather. One raises its head and stares at him. Carol liked ponies. She moved slowly when she was near them and held out her hand for them to sniff and wasn't frightened when they snorted and threw up their heads. When she was older she sometimes rode a friend's pony, but most things they did together. He taught her how to dam streams and to climb trees, holding out his hand to help her when she gazed trustingly up at him. Her hair was brown and curly like his; anyone could see they were brother and sister.

Perhaps Carol's house will have a view of Dartmoor. Perhaps he will be able to walk on the moor, during the day, because there would not be many people there. In Birmingham he always walked at night, keeping to better-lit streets and avoiding the railway bridges and the banks of the canal where the cider drinkers and drug addicts gathered. In the evenings he and Carol could sit together and talk about the past or watch television together. He could get books from the library to read.

A signpost points down a side road to Tarr Steps. They had been there, surely, as children! He remembers running across a river on flat stones and eating a picnic on the broad green banks. He sits down on the soft turf to eat an apple and study the road atlas. He needs to go further west and following this road will help. Here, the moor is as he remembered it in his childhood; bright green closely-grazed turf, undulating and hummocky, scattered with small hawthorn trees hung with pale-green lichen. Every step he takes is taking him closer to Carol and the chance of leading a meaningful life.

The narrow lane leads down into the river valley. There is a lot of traffic so he pulls his hood further forward and frequently has to press himself against the hedge to allow cars to pass, turning his face away from the curious stares. A man shouts from a car window,

'You warm enough, mate!'

It is a comment, that is all; no harm is meant, so he keeps his head down and breathes deeply in the way Tessa showed him. Then almost at once there is a car park and people walking in front of him and behind him, all heading for the river and the bridge of flat stones. He glimpses men and women in shorts sitting on the grass and children in swimsuits running in and out of the water; he walks straight across the bridge and up into the coppiced oak woodland above, to a secluded spot where he can eat and, later, pitch his tent. Only when the sun has left the valley and the voices have ceased, does he walk slowly down the shadowy path to the river. When he is sure he is alone, he crouches under the sheltering trees and washes his hands and face in the pure running water, washing and rinsing until all the grime is gone and he is clean. Then he stands on the primitive stone bridge, staring at the water that flows ceaselessly over the stony bed and remembering the past, and he knows with a deep certainty that he will find that contentment again.

The next morning he can already hear people at Tarr Steps as he packs up his tent and walks through the wood to the lane. The slanting rays of the sun are warming the dew-laden verges, drawing from them a haze of steam that hangs in the air at shoulder-height. He picks cow wheat and field scabious and then a perfect dog rose. He will find another, closer to Okehampton so that it will be fresh, and give it to Carol when she opens the door to him. He puts the rose in the buttonhole of his parka and looks down at it now and again as he walks. It reminds him of her; its sweet old-fashioned innocence.

The lane winds up and out of the river valley until he is again on the open moor and soon he reaches a straight tree-lined road that runs along the top of a ridge. At his back is the wild brown moorland; before him a meadow drops rapidly away and Devon is displayed below, a huge carpet of emerald fields etched with hedges into every shape imaginable and patched with darker green woodland, stretching as far as the eye can see. And there, on the horizon, is the shadowy bulk of Dartmoor rising solidly from the grasslands. Okehampton is close by and in two or three days he will be there. He will find the street and the number of her house and he will knock and she will open the door. Carol. His sister, smiling.

'Come in!' she will say.

'Come in!'

The Whale

Rose was squeezed between Kirsty's sharp little elbow and the car door. Her view of the North Devon Link Road was obscured by the headrest, and the smell of new plastic was already making her feel nauseous.

'Are you all right back there, Rose? Not too squashed?'

'No, 'tis lovely, thank you. Beautiful. We're nice and cosy, aren't we, Kirsty?'

Kirsty was arguing with her sister and did not answer. From the driving seat, Ellen continued her conversation with her grandson, who had to sit in the front in case he was sick. Rose looked out of the side window, concentrating on the distant hills so her stomach wasn't upset by the verge fizzing past. It was very hot, but she was too cramped to be able to take off her cardigan and if she opened the window, her hair blew all over her face. The weather had been hot all week. She had to have the windows open at home and then the continuous drone of the forage harvesters and the deafening clatter of the silage trailers nearly drove her mad. That was one of the drawbacks of having a bungalow right on the edge of the estate. When the noise stopped the day before yesterday, the sudden silence was even worse.

Rose had noticed in previous years that there can be a lull in the middle of August when the weather at last settles; when the cars that converge on the county have arrived and the visitors are all on the beach; when the last cut of silage is completed and the empty yellow fields lie peacefully under an azure sky; when the wheat is ripening and the maize is growing taller and every day is hotter than the one before. Usually it was a time to treasure.

She looked out at the golden landscape from the car window and hated it. She shouldn't have come. Ellen had only asked her because she felt sorry for her. 'I'm taking the children to Lynton and Lynmouth for the day and we'd love you to come with us. It'd do you good to get out.' She'd smiled sympathetically over the garden fence. What was there to feel sorry for anyway?

Rose had planned to have days out once Doug retired. She thought they could go out at least one day a week; drive to Ilfracombe and walk along the harbour, to Exeter to look around the shops or perhaps to Combe Martin because she hadn't been there for years. She had thought that having occasional days out would give her something to talk about, which could otherwise be difficult when you had no family. Ellen could talk about all sorts of things because, having children and grandchildren, she had kept up. She even had a computer.

'Sophie, give it *here, now*!' Kirsty stepped hard on Rose's toe as she lunged over to snatch the phone from her sister.

'Girls! Let poor Rose have some peace and quiet in the back there!'

'Oh, I'm all right. 'Tis lovely to have their company.'

As they started to go round the interminable Barnstaple roundabouts, first the door handle and then Kirsty's elbow pressed into her side. Ellen drove too fast; Doug always used to say so. The girls were singing a pop song together, very loudly and out of tune, to compete with the relentlessly cheerful voices of Radio Devon on the car radio. They had been lovely children when they were little but now the girls were almost teenagers, they seemed to bicker all the time and talk about things Rose didn't understand. Ellen had her hands full, having the three of them to stay.

Rose's legs were prickling with the heat but if she left off her tights, her veins looked ugly. She ought to walk more. Usually she walked into Bideford to do the shopping or to drink tea with her friend in the café that had been in Mill Street ever since she was a girl, but in the five weeks since *it* happened, she'd hardly been out at all. She felt the perspiration trickling down the back of her neck and she pictured her living room, all neat and tidy with a nice cool breeze rustling the curtains. How stupid of her to come. It was all Doug's fault. She wouldn't be here if he was still alive.

She *told* him he should go to the doctor. Did he ever listen? 'It may *not* be indigestion,' she told him, 'if you won't go for your own sake, then at least you could go for mine!' He just mumbled something and disappeared into the spare room to play around with his model farm. When did he ever think of her? It was just the same all those years ago; she'd *pleaded* with him to go to the doctor then, but he wouldn't. If he'd seen a doctor about that difficulty years ago, she might have children and grandchildren now. It was *his* fault she was all on her own with no family to care for. To have a grandchild to hold on your lap, a little cherub with curly hair who looks up into your face! Who says, 'Look, Nanny! Look!' Who crouches on the lawn and picks daisies and gives them to you with the stems all crumpled! But he wouldn't go to the doctor, so now there were no family gatherings with children running around, no Christmases around the tree to look forward to, but only her brother and his wife with their complaints and their dreadful neighbours.

And if he'd gone to the doctor last month, she wouldn't have had to find him on the spare room floor like that. The shock of it! As she walked into the room there'd been that curious silence, thick and heavy, then the sight of him lying there, flat out, so that she'd thought for a moment that he was fooling around. She had been angry ever since, far too angry to cry.

'Oh, look at that view! Rose, can you see? The countryside is such a picture! Look, children!'

Rose could only see an occasional glimpse of the steep valley as the car wound sickeningly down the hairpin bends.

'Beautiful! I'm so glad you asked me, Ellen.'

The car sped past dusty hedges festooned with wisps of straw from one of the laden trailers they had met on a bend. Doug had always been interested in farming. He'd spent a good part of his time on that model farm and had said he wished he could rent a small field and keep a few sheep when he retired. Ridiculous. He'd no sense at all.

'A field!' she'd said. 'You could start by cutting the lawn a bit more often.'

She tried, yesterday, to make a start on turning out his clothes because some of them were so old she was ashamed to have them in the house.

'You're *not* wearing that!' she used to say. 'Don't think I'm going to be seen out with you looking like that!'

He wouldn't throw them out. Then there were the new things still in their wrappings, brand new cricketing clothes, because he'd once had a fancy to play cricket but was not chosen for the team. And a shirt he had never worn because he thought it rather too bright. Such a waste! It made her so cross.

There was a lot of clearing out to do but somehow she couldn't get on with it. She tried, but then would sit down, and somehow an hour or more would pass.

The car turned into the car park in Lynton and the children leapt out. Rose's legs had stiffened up. She got out slowly and looked around. It was a long time since she had visited Lynton but she could remember those stone-built villas and the green hill running up behind. It used to remind her of Switzerland, not that she'd ever been there, because she could never persuade Doug to leave England.

'Other people go abroad,' she used to say, 'everyone we know goes abroad apart from us.'

Ellen was walking towards the main street with the children and Rose trailed along behind. The narrow street was lined with old stone houses with steeply-pitched tiled roofs and little balconies. Nearly all of them had shop fronts with goods spilling out on to the pavement; wicker baskets and leather bags, racks of postcards and tubs full of shells. It wasn't as pretty as she remembered. There were people everywhere and you could hardly get along the pavement.

'Please Gran, can I have one of those bags? They're so cool!'

Ellen went into one of the shops with the children and Rose stood outside. Nearly all of the passers-by had shoulders and backs burnt red by the sun and many seemed to have northern accents, which she had never been fond of. She watched a tall, badly-dressed girl with a small dumpy man in shorts, an oddly-matched couple who, from the look on their faces, seemed surprised to find themselves on honeymoon together. When she and Doug had been on honeymoon they'd never been like that; she'd been proud to be seen with him. They'd strolled along arm-in-arm in Torquay and people had looked at them because they made an impression. They had their whole lives in front of them. She'd never dreamed things would turn out the way they did. Ellen was still in the shop with the children, looking at animals made from shells, so Rose moved into the shade and tried to focus on some postcards. Above the rooftops a flock of jackdaws wheeled and flapped and cried to each other pointlessly.

Ellen and the children went in another gift shop, then in a shop selling paintings.

'I think we could do with some lunch now, don't you? Would something light suit you, Rose? Some sandwiches perhaps?'

'Oh, I'd love a sandwich, thank you! That'd just do for me.'

The café was busy and they shuffled on to some benches around a table designed for four. The tables were so cramped that a tattooed man in a vest almost knocked Rose's tea over when he sat down and she had to listen to him swearing about the traffic jams and the cost of the car parks while she ate her ham sandwich. He really should have considered the children even if he didn't care about her. Doug almost never swore and if he did, he apologised.

'Auntie Rose, we're going on the cliff railway now!' Kirsty took her hand and almost pulled her along. They went along a processional high-walled way decorated with bright hanging baskets and came to a viewpoint over Lynmouth Bay where a crowd of visitors exclaimed and held up their phones to take pictures. The children wriggled into the throng to get to the front and she was pulled in by Kirsty.

'Wow, Auntie Rose, look at that! The sea's so blue!'

'You can see for miles! How many miles can you see, Gran? Are we going all the way down there?'

Rose stared out at the emptiness. In the sea, past the expanse of grey pebbles, the black shapes of surfers floated just beyond the white-topped waves like hideous birds, waiting.

They stood in a long queue behind a white chain link fence for their turn to board the railcar. They shuffled forwards very slowly and Rose's legs began to ache. A green-painted railcar glided up out of nowhere, a bored-looking man stepped out and there was a sound of gushing water.

'Look, kids, that's the water tank filling up,' said Ellen. At last they all stepped into the little green box and the man indicated that Rose should sit down. Ellen and the children went on to the outside platform, blocking the view for everyone in the car. A bell rang and the car rocked a little then started to sink between ivy-grown stone walls. 'Whee, down we go!' said a woman. There was a rattle of cables and a wheezing sound as they passed straight down through the narrow passage cut into the cliff face, down between high walls of damp vegetation where the sun could not penetrate. It seemed absurd to place trust in such an apparently perilous descent; they must be dropping hundreds of feet. Rose tried not to meet the eyes of the people sitting opposite; it was rather like sitting on the London Underground except people attempted to smile because they were on holiday. When it stopped they all stood up and walked out in single file. There was a smell of seaweed and fish and chips.

They stood by the sea wall and looked out at the waves. Ellen lifted her grandson up and kissed him extravagantly.

'Can we go in the sea, Gran? Did you bring our swimming things?'

'The beach here isn't the best for swimming but we could go to Westward Ho! tomorrow.

Are you all right, Rose? Enjoying yourself?' She gave Rose a hug and whispered to her. 'Don't worry; I know it's difficult for you.'

'No, I'm *fine*. I'm really enjoying myself!'

She leaned forward with her arms folded on the wall and stared at the horizon, like a seasick passenger. The sound of the surf seemed to get louder, as if it would drown her.

Gradually she became aware of the voices of the people around her.

'It's enormous!'

'So sad! You have to see it.'

'Rose? There's a whale, further up on the beach. We're going to walk along and see it. Will you come?'

They walked along the front and through the car park at the foot of the cliff. Rose followed. A crowd of people were standing by the sea wall staring out on to the beach and talking quietly. Then she saw it. A massive grey shape on the grey pebbles; a huge creature the size of a bus. It was lying quite motionless. She saw its notched tail and her gaze travelled up the whole length of its body and she saw its deep, intelligent eye.

It was so very still. So very sad.

'Is it dead?' She spoke in a whisper. A man replied.

'Yes, it's dead.' His voice, too, was very quiet.

She had seen a film about a whale; a gentle, sensuous animal whose very existence seemed miraculous; an ancient, perceptive being with a haunting voice and a humorous smile that played intricate games, gliding through the ocean and rising to the surface to stand vertically in the water, slapping its tail and blowing triumphantly; a gentle creature that never turns on man, however harshly it is treated. A vital, living being. And here it was; lifeless. Broken. So huge and out of place, lying there in the glare of the sun; such a sudden, unexpected sight, and pity for the whale welled up within her and overwhelmed her and there was a roaring in her ears and the pebbles on the beach and the blue sea beyond grew misty and indistinct.

'Rose? Rose, are you all right? Rose, darling.'

And Ellen's arms were around her and she realised that tears were streaming down her face.

Somehow she managed to speak.

'I'll be all right. I think I must be on my own for a while.'

She walked back by the sea wall, through the dark doorway of the old tower that stood by the harbour, out in the sun again and right to the end of the harbour wall. She leaned on the wall and looked blindly out to sea and sobs wracked her body until she could barely draw breath. She cried for the whale that lay so still and helpless on the beach and she cried for Doug, her wonderful, vital, loving husband who had gone for ever and who she missed so much, so very much. Her love for him surged within her, slow and huge like a whale rising from the water, rising up and up, a thing of beauty and grandeur, and with her love came pity for the life that had ended so abruptly, and so alone.

She could not tell how long she stood there. She became aware of people who passed close by and considerately left her alone, and a woman who placed a hand on her arm and quietly offered help. Gradually her body began to quieten and as her tears flowed more slowly, the memories came back; standing by a sea wall such as this and Doug coming up behind her and putting his arms around her and holding an ice cream to her lips which she could hardly eat for laughing; taking her hand on holiday in Cornwall, hesitantly, because by then they had been married many years and hand-holding was becoming rare, and treasured all the more for that; sitting together in the conservatory at home and thinking, yes, we will be retired and we will be happy right into old age, despite our occasional differences.

She raised her head and looked out at the sheer grass-topped cliffs curving round the perfect blue bay and she saw the surfers. They rose on their boards as the wave came and they rode the ridges and the furrows of the sea, twisting and turning with perfect balance and such graceful freedom. How

Doug would have loved to watch them! She could hear his voice as if he were here beside her,

'Just look at them, Rose! I would have loved to learn to surf.'

Poor Doug. There were so many things he would have liked to do.

'I miss you, Doug', she whispered. 'I miss you, my wonderful boy.'

She turned, and there was the busy waterfront and the perfect cottages garlanded with flowers, the semicircle of steep wooded hillsides behind and the river running from the wooded ravines in a reassuring, continuous flow over the pebbles to the sea.

'You should be here, seeing this, Doug.'

Ellen was sitting on a seat on the far side of the harbour, watching and waiting with her curly-haired grandson on her lap, and the girls sat on a wall, studying the phone together and swinging their tanned legs. She looked the other way, to the still, sad sight of the body on the beach, then she walked towards the waterfront and Ellen rose to greet her and Kirsty jumped down from the wall to take her hand.

She held Rose's hand all the way home as they drove through the glowing countryside. Exhausted, Rose declined the offer of tea and Ellen hugged her and asked if she was sure she would be all right alone. She wandered through the silent house and opened Doug's wardrobe, stroking the neatly hanging clothes and inhaling their scent and letting the tears come again. She opened the door of the spare room and saw the perfect farmyard laid out on boards, the model barns and fences he had so lovingly constructed, the tractors and the sheep in the fields he had painted with an enthusiasm she had never allowed him to share. Then she went to the cabinet and took out the photograph albums and a bundle of letters tied with a ribbon, letters he had written to her when they were engaged. She settled down to read them for the first time in over thirty years.

That night she dreamed of Doug and the honeymoon in Torquay. They were in the sea together, she in that old swimsuit which went baggy in the water, he in those closely-fitting trunks that are no longer fashionable. He dived under the waves, a huge shadowy shape moving slowly under the water, and she felt her feet being tickled and she shrieked, almost falling, helpless with laughter. When he surfaced with water streaming from his hair and his face alive with pleasure, they laughed and embraced, their bodies wet and slippery from the sea and their mouths meeting. They held each other close and together they dived and glided effortlessly through the water, their limbs entangling so that they became one living body, she and Doug together, a graceful creature slipping deeper and deeper, away from the glare of the sun and down to the depths of the ocean.

The Gardener

Where will he be today? Each week when Hilary arrives at Rosemoor, she walks right around the gardens until she sees him. She makes herself walk slowly like all the other visitors so as not to attract attention to herself, and when she sees him digging in the vegetable garden or using his secateurs in the exotic garden, she turns calmly away to find a seat. The seat must be carefully selected. It must be behind him and a little distance away, preferably at an angle so she has to turn her head to see him. She would not want him to feel that he is under scrutiny.

The low September sun gives out gentle warmth and accentuates the pinks, mauves and creams of the long border. The cannas are fully open today; regal in bearing, they glow with the colour of butter against the backdrop of the wooded hillside beyond. Every week at Rosemoor there are subtle changes wrought by time and weather. She has observed the variations each week since June.

She hadn't expected to come here so often. She thought that they would be able to talk on that very first visit, but the weeks have passed and she is still visiting every Thursday and is still waiting. That is all she can do, wait, and return each week so that he knows she will never give up on him. She pauses at the top of the steps to see the immaculate acres laid out before her. She will walk through the formal gardens, where every turn past the high yew hedges gives a new vista and a reason for anticipation, and if he's not there she will walk through the stream field, down to the lake and on to the fruit and vegetable garden.

On her first visit she strode feverishly through the garden without looking at it. She attracted a good deal of attention. When she found him she delivered the speech she had rehearsed, but he resolutely turned his back on her, defeating

93

her attempts at calmness until her increasingly desperate pleas resulted in him abandoning the lawn edge he was manicuring and walking quickly away. The same thing happened the following week, except she lost control and screamed at his departing back. The next time, she left a carefully-worded letter on the bench close to where he was working. For a week afterwards she waited for a phone call or at least a text message in response. She realised then that it was going to take longer than she had thought, so she filled in the forms to become a member of the Royal Horticultural Society giving her free entry to Rosemoor, and she sketched him digging, pouring love into every line of the pencil and leaving the sketch on the bench at the end of the day. Another week she left a chocolate cake in a tin labelled with his name, then an iridescent jay's feather, and later a new paperback. She never knew whether he picked them up or what became of them.

She pauses to take in the cool, pastel colours of the spiral garden and watches a tall, silver-haired woman discussing hydrangeas with her husband. It was on her fourth or fifth visit that she began to notice other people. At Rosemoor, people move slowly and speak quietly. There is no anger; no raised voices. They stroll and look all about them as if they have walked out of their usual lives and into an enchanted place, a Garden of Eden. Middle-aged couples hold hands. Babies new to walking stumble across the grass, eyes and mouth wide open with delight at this adventure of a lawn that goes on for ever. Men in suits take their mothers' arms and patiently point out the floribundas. Hilary watched them and matched her pace to theirs. She noted their appearance and realised how wild she must have looked on that first visit. She saw how they contemplated their surroundings and she made her gaze follow theirs. She used to consider the visiting of gardens to be the preserve of retired people with generous pensions, people who had nothing more worthwhile to do than to stroll, and admire, and declare 'Oh, how lovely!' but gradually Rosemoor began to work its magic on her, too. Now, each week when she arrives, she sees the perfectly proportioned steps inviting her down into the formal area, she notices the immaculate hedges enclosing the jewels of the rose garden and she appreciates the soothing sound of running water drawing her to the terrace garden. Now she strolls like everyone else; it is no longer pretence. She has felt well enough to go back to work, part-time. It is not easy dealing with human misery again and trying to solve problems that go back generations, visiting chaotic households where the only communication is a shout, or a scream, but she is staying calm, and she is coping. It's a life-saver for her really, coming here.

Today is her birthday. When she looks back over the year, she can only feel relief that it is over. She went out for dinner yesterday evening with three friends, good friends who have stood by her despite everything, and they tried to reassure her that the coming year would be better. Will Tom remember that it is her birthday? As she walks down across the stream field, she pauses for a moment by the grand old oak and imagines that it bows to her a little to wish her many happy returns of the day. Is there something different about this day, a particular stillness, a sense of things awaiting fruition? The leaves of the yellow birch, Betula Lutea, are turning to gold and bronze and beginning to fall, the first to do so. She didn't know the names of any plants when she first came in June, but there are many things she has learned since then. Sometimes she writes down the Latin names and looks them up on the internet when she gets home. It is a new language for her; a gentle, forgiving language pertaining to naming and understanding. One could never use the name of a tree in anger or accusation.

A motorised buggy is approaching along the path. She sees Tom, in the passenger seat, wearing his green trousers with padded knees, his secateurs and walkie-talkie bulging from the pockets, his dark green shirt. The buggy draws near. It is driven by a man she believes to be his boss, an older man with a calm, patient face who smiles rather sadly at her as they pass. Tom looks straight ahead, his gaze fixed on the distant horizon. Tom. Her son. She carefully maintains her slow pace although she feels shaky and a little faint. How did he look? So boyish, still, at twenty-one. His untidy blonde hair. His lankiness in the confined space of the buggy. Had he looked troubled, the way he did sometimes as a toddler, that look that used to so easily change to an open smile when she called his name?

She leans on the little wooden bridge, her heart pounding, and tries to focus on the view of the lake framed by the two old oaks and the red-topped liquidambar; it is an image of such glowing perfection in the September sunlight that its beauty overwhelms her and she has to look away. If he is unhappy, it is her fault. He must dislike her intensely if he cannot even bear to look at her! Below the bridge the water runs endlessly down the stepped stream path and she cries for the past and for a future she cannot fathom.

When she first visited, her intention had been to make her peace with him or, if she couldn't do that, simply to be near him, but as the weeks passed she found that something else was happening. She watched him working and, gradually, she began to understand him. She saw that the adolescent who had sometimes exasperated her had gone. She saw that he was passionate about his work, that it absorbed him so much, he sometimes forgot her presence. Whether he was sweeping a path or digging in the vegetable garden, he worked with fervent concentration and she remembered that, in truth, he had always done so. There was time for reflection in the long hours spent sitting on benches and many memories returned to her; Tom as a toddler, busy with an excavation in the sandpit; an earnest eight-year-old Tom with dirty knees, trying to build a dry stone wall at the end of the garden and calling out for help; a gangly thirteen-year-old engrossed in his homework, his voice breaking as he turned and replied to her question, making them both laugh. Her Tom, now a confident, independent adult. She saw that he was part of a team of employees and volunteers dedicated to ensuring that for the visitors the view of the garden is perfect from every angle. They sweep the paths, mow the lawns, plan, prune and trim, creating a stage set where people may saunter and be captivated. Tom was a skilled member of this team; she heard him having a mild disagreement with another gardener over summer pruning, and was startled by his persuasive approach and authoritative use of terms she did not understand – espalier, sub-laterals and secondary growth. The other gardener, a young man as short and thick-set as Tom was tall and lean, was won over and now the pear tree flourished against the old stone wall and the fruit grew large and ripened early, due to his skill. She drew it lovingly for him, and the deep apricot dahlias that he had staked so carefully, and left the drawings on a bench. As the summer reached its height and she learned to appreciate the beauty that his devotion helped to create, she gradually realised just how much she had failed him. She had not hidden her disappointment when he chose what she called manual labour instead of academic study, and she was openly dismissive of his college course; she allowed herself to be distracted by her work and took no interest in his, was so short with him when he tried to talk to her that eventually he no longer told her anything. She lost sight of her son, rarely considering his misery as she and his father battled around him. She said unwarranted, wounding things, and she cries now when she remembers his dear face struggling to hide the hurt behind a mask of indifference. It was not surprising that he took his father's side; it was all she deserved. He has not spoken to her since the day she moved out.

She walks down the path to the water's edge. The lake is motionless and glassy, reflecting its complex green backdrop. The two women who were sitting on the seat have left and for a while the silence is complete but for an occasional plop as a fish jumps, sending ripples towards the clusters of water lilies. A large, dark green dragonfly hovers, glides, and hovers again with an uncanny persistence. The trees stand mute and expectant. Surely one day Tom will speak to her. Where is he now? If he is having his lunch he will be unlikely to return for a while; she may as well go to the restaurant. She rises from the seat, although she is not hungry.

She carries her sandwich and her coffee out to the courtyard and sits at one of the octagonal wooden tables, noticing once more how many absences they create for someone sitting alone. People sitting at other tables converse comfortably, and are relaxed when silences develop. A tall man with a white beard leans towards her, smiling; 'Sunshine!' he says, as a passing cloud goes on its way. She smiles politely and quickly looks away. A few chaffinches and a single robin hop beneath the tables looking for crumbs and occasionally fly up to regard the occupants quizzically, heads on one side. She drinks her coffee. There is a book in her bag but she does not feel like reading.

She makes herself take a circuitous route before going to the vegetable garden. He must have come from there because there was a box of apples, some cabbages and some onions in the back of the buggy, being taken to the restaurant perhaps. He may be working there all day. He may be working with the young gardener with the pretty dark hair. Once she heard them laughing together as they worked and was afraid she might be intruding, so she went home early. She hadn't minded because it was such a pleasure to see him enjoying himself. She wishes she could ask him about his work: whether every day is different or whether he works for a week in one area; what he likes doing best and whether his boss is as kind as he looks. When she was able to ask him, she never thought to do so.

She chooses an old lichen-grown bench above the orchard overlooking the path Tom will follow to reach the fruit and vegetable garden. The low, spreading branches in the orchard are laden with apples; russet, green, crimson, yellow and deep pink fruit gleam against the azure sky. A red admiral, a perfect composition in black and white and burnt orange, flutters back and forth beneath the trees as if searching for something, alighting briefly on an apple from time to time before continuing its quest. She watches, and turns her head each time a new figure comes into view on the path, but she sees only strolling visitors, no lanky young man wearing green clothes. Perhaps she is mistaken and he will not be returning to this area. Finally she crosses the grass to enter the vegetable garden and admire his work.

There are six varieties of corn salad and six of radish; perfect lines of pak choi and mizuna; enormous orange and pale yellow pumpkins nestling among big round leaves. In a fruit cage large autumn raspberries ripen on immaculate canes; raspberries have always been her favourite; what a treat it would be to have them so late in the year. Guiltily she pushes her fingers through the wire netting but the fruit are just beyond her reach. She wanders along the path, admiring the row of bright orange marigolds and the flawless onions and then she hears the careful scrape, scrape, scrape of a hoe. It is Tom, facing slightly away from her, gently controlling the long handle of the hoe. She takes a step or two back. There is nowhere to sit. If she moves back a few more feet, she can stand behind the canes where tightly spiralled stems bear a few late runner beans. There; she can see him through the leaves. He is leaning on the handle now and gazing into the distance, his hair falling into his eyes. He turns and almost looks in her direction, then resumes his work. Is he rather distracted? He has surely worked that piece of ground for long enough. He stops work again and looks around, a quick glance towards the orchard, then almost this way again. Could he have seen her sitting by the apple trees? He must have been working here while she was waiting for him to come along the path. She longs to step out from behind the canes and call across to him.

If she stays here, hiding, she will risk annoying him, because it is not the same as sitting on a seat in full view; he will feel she is spying on him. She will have to find a seat even if it is some distance away. She steps out from behind the runner beans and suddenly he turns and looks straight at her and puts up his hand. He means her to stop. He is afraid she will come closer. It is a hesitant movement and, if she could have set aside all that had happened in the last year, she might almost have thought it to be a greeting. She turns and walks slowly away from him. When she reaches the gate, she looks back. He is standing very straight, watching her. For a moment that feels like an hour, they gaze at each other, then she turns and walks on. She takes steady, measured steps to try to control the ridiculous fit of shaking that has come over her. She is glad that he was too far away for her to see his expression, for it was sure to have been contemptuous.

Beyond are wooden gates which bear a sign, '*No Unauthorised Persons Beyond This Point*'. She can see coiled hoses, stacked pots and rows of wheelbarrows neatly lined up on their sides. There are days when he spends time in there, out of her sight. Sometimes she hears the sound of machines and once he came out wearing ear defenders. She imagined they were to shut out the sound of her voice. There is a seat nearby and she sits with her closed book on her lap.

A long hour passes. Now that the day is almost over, the disappointment at not being able to talk with Tom weighs very heavy. Why had she imagined that today might be the day? She does not deserve to speak to him, but having so little opportunity on her birthday even to see him is hard to bear. Autumn is coming, and then winter. Will it be too cold to sit outside near Tom? What will she do when it is raining? She makes herself rise and walk to the restaurant for a cup of tea. Before she leaves Rosemoor, she will return to the bench to leave the flapjacks she has made for him.

She walks the long way around to the restaurant, past the new children's playground in the woods. There is a teacher and a group of seven- or eight-year-olds in jeans and wellingtons, shouting excitedly over the carved wooden sculptures, running in and out of the willow house and playing elaborate chasing games between the trees. One boy is balancing carefully on the upturned logs; his curly hair and focussed concentration remind her somewhat of Tom. When another child joins him, he looks up and she sees an open face and a spontaneous, welcoming smile that changes to an expression of mock alarm as he almost loses his footing.

How easy life had been when Tom was young! Her birthdays had always been such happy days. Her marriage was good enough then, but it was Tom who thought up treats for her, one year making her a picnic which they ate together in the park, another year – he would only have been about seven – presenting her with a little chest of drawers he had made from matchboxes glued together and decorated. She still keeps her earrings in it.

She sits in the half-empty restaurant with her cup of tea, hearing the staff chatting and laughing behind the counter. It is a wonder that they can be so caught up in the minutiae of their work, that there can be so much purpose and movement. If only she could be thinking of her evening, planning for tomorrow or writing a shopping list, but all she can think of is Tom; imagine him sitting opposite her, his gentle, humorous voice, his warm smile, the smell of him. *I want you back; I want you back; Tom, I'm sorry for all I said. I won't ask too much of you, just to see you sometimes and talk with you. Come back to me, Tom.* The longing for him is so intense, she can hardly draw breath. The two women behind the counter are watching her. She realises she is crying.

She walks slowly back through the garden. The sun is casting long shadows and the temperature has fallen. She pulls her cardigan around her shoulders and walks with her arms folded across her chest and her head down. In the herb garden the low sun catches the golden seed heads of fennel and the dry, downcast faces of the sunflowers, brought to fruition by the long summer days. She trails her hand over the leathery leaves of the sage bush to release the spicy aroma. Her pace has slowed still further; she is reluctant to reach the bench by the staff area, to put down the bag of flapjacks for Tom, then turn and walk away. She makes herself continue, past the oak, over the stream.

There is something on the bench already. Confused, she puts her hand in her bag, but can feel that the flapjacks are still there. She gets closer, staring at the bench – could someone else have left something for Tom? It is a flat, woven basket lined with leaves like a nest and on the leaves is a mound of autumn raspberries and a note. She reads '*For Mum. Love from Tom.*' There is a movement and she looks up, her eyes swimming, and he is there, standing by the gate with the sleeves of his shirt rolled up and his hair falling in his eyes, and for a long moment they look at each other and she sees that there is no anger in his face, only uncertainty and distress. Then he is taking a step forward and she is too, and even when he is close, she is unable to speak because she is charged with love.

'Mum, I'm sorry, I'm so sorry.' His voice is breaking a little with emotion and he is holding out his arms to her. 'Happy Birthday, Mum.'

Harvest Gold

It all started with a bag of flour. I was strolling up the High Street and deciding it wasn't worth applying for a part-time job I'd seen advertised in the window of the off-licence. Most part-time jobs around here pay less than job-seeker's and if I had to serve those drunks who sit by the river eyeing up every woman who walks by, there was no way I was doing it for nothing. I prefer care work and knew I'd pick up some more before long. Anyway, it was then that I noticed the flour. It was in one of those shops that appear overnight selling off tacky ornaments and random clothes and close again after a few weeks. This one had some plastic flowers in eye-watering colours, a pile of pink and white striped shorts that were big enough to go around me at least three times, and an enormous blue furry rabbit. That was all in one window. The other window was full of flour.

I make my own bread. Just because I'm unemployed doesn't mean I have to live on ready meals that probably contain horsemeat. I've always found it weird that other people live like that; I mean, these instant things are actually more expensive than proper food and when you're not working you've got the time to cook. I make my own soup from the bags of bruised veggies the greengrocer sells for like 10p and I got a load of apples just by asking an old lady up the road because she couldn't pick them herself. So what with that and some bits and pieces that some of the guys skip from round the back of the supermarket, I do all right really. I don't need for anything.

I'd forgotten to buy flour so when I saw this big notice, '*Wholemeal Bread Flour, £1 a bag*,' well, it seemed too good to miss. After all, flour is flour, or so I thought. I went into the shop and Megan waited outside, watching me the way she does with her ears standing up like butterfly wings. She's a lurcher, long-haired, with more than a pinch of collie in her.

'Nice dog you've got. Can't keep his eyes off you, can he?'

The man in the shop was a bit leery and unhealthy-looking so I wasn't going to hang around.

'She.' I said. 'I want to get a bag of flour.' He got the message.

I had a look at the bag when I got back to my room and I thought it was a bit unusual. They always try to make processed foods look natural and home produced, like fresh from the country and all that kind of thing, but it did cross my mind that this was the genuine article. Anyway I thought no more about it until the next day when I decided to make bread.

Me and Megan go for a walk every day, usually with Zoe and Tubs and their dogs, and in ten minutes we can be out of the town and in the real countryside. It's cool because it keeps me fit and reminds me of the natural order of things, and I can turn off the heating while I'm out so I save a couple of hours of electricity which means I can afford to meet the others when there's a good band in the Bell on a Friday night. Early October was perfect: heavy dew on the grass when we went out early, spiders' webs shining as if spun from silver thread, the last few swallows passing overhead and in the woods the first leaves just beginning to fall and acorns crunching under our feet. Sometimes we picked blackberries or fungi. Most days we walked up through the woods to the twenty acre field so we could let the dogs have a run and they would chase each other round and round in ever bigger circles, right over to the far side. The farmer lets us go in there when it's not being grazed because he appreciated how I looked after his mum when she was dying.

Well, on this particular morning it was pissing down with rain so I decided to leave the walk until later and bake some bread. I opened the packet and started shaking the flour out into a bowl. It was really coarse. I picked out one or two husks but as I shook out a bit more, there were little bits of straw then a whole grain which hadn't been crushed at all. This was weird; I mean you usually pay a lot more for food which has had less done to it, like organic apples and that kind of thing, but this flour was well cheap. I decided I might as well try it as it was without picking out the really coarse bits, so I tipped the bag right up. Out came more straw, more whole grains, then - somehow I sensed there was something more solid in there and when I stopped pouring and peered into the bag, I could see a little ball of straw and something moving inside it. I dropped the bag on the table and leapt back. A faint rustling came from the packet. I thought of cockroaches and dirty kitchens and stifled a desire to run right out of the room, then I braced myself, crept over to the table and peered into the packet.

A little face stared back at me. A small, brown, furry face with bright, black eyes and long whiskers. When I jumped, the face did too and disappeared back into the flour. Well, by then my heart was racing and I felt kind of shaky all over; I had to go and sit down as far away from the table as possible and reason with myself. OK, so there was an animal in my flour. It wasn't going to hurt me; I didn't have to use the flour; all I had to do was find out what it was and then, well, I could decide what to do about it later. I pussyfooted back to the table and ever so slowly leaned forward until I could see into the bag. And there it was. Sitting up on its haunches, washing the flour from its face with quick, precise movements of its delicate little feet. I knew what it was because I'd seen one a few times when I was a kid and used to play in the hay bales on my friend's farm. My bag of flour was home to a harvest mouse.

I didn't feel so bad once I'd identified it. It was a shame I couldn't use the flour because it would have been interesting to see what the bread would have been like with all that roughage in it, but there were quite a lot of droppings so it didn't seem a very good idea. The problem was, what to do with the mouse. I didn't want him running round in my room;

Megan's really gentle but I didn't think I could trust her with a mouse and the more I saw of him, the less I wanted him to get hurt. I couldn't just release him outside because the cars speed up this road like it's some kind of race track, and then there are all the cats. No. He was a harvest mouse and he belonged in the country where he could be killed naturally by an owl or a fox, though to be honest I was beginning to wonder whether he might be immortal, because I could hardly imagine the dangers he must have survived before ending up in this bag. I looked at him again. He was really cute. Rusty brown with a white tummy, long whiskers and tail, neat round ears and those black eyes which gleamed at me. He looked quite fat, contented really, and not frightened of me anymore. I found an old shoebox, pierced some holes in the lid, and put some crumpled newspaper in the bottom along with a handful of flour to make him feel more at home. Of course he could chew his way out if he wanted but he hadn't tried to escape from the bag. I picked him up and he looked a bit surprised and started washing his face in a nervous, jerky way but he soon settled down when he was in the box. I'd got some seeds because I use lots in cooking, so I gave him some sunflower and pumpkin seeds. I expect he was glad of the change.

It wasn't until later that I looked more closely at the flour bag. The more I thought things through, the more freaked out I got. I mean, assuming this mouse was in the wheat when it was harvested, how had it survived all the mechanical processes - not that I knew much about them, that changes a field of wheat into bags of flour? I should really have gone down to Trading Standards or Environmental Health or somewhere like that but I fancied doing a bit of detective work of my own. And where could I start but with the now empty bag? It was handwritten rather than printed; *Wholemeal Bread Flour* it said, *100% Natural* - it was certainly that - then there were some rather badly-drawn ears of wheat and on the back a name, *D. Wheeler*, and the name of a farm near Bransworthy. So the next day I put an elastic band round the shoe box and headed down the bus stop.

It's only about ten miles to Bransworthy but I'd never been there before. The bus brings old biddies into town in the morning to shop and drives them back to the village at twelve, and when I got on, everyone was chatting together and joking with the driver. I got some funny looks at first – it's the nose ring and tattoo that does it – but then I got talking to the old man next to me and he was amazing, told me about the farms he used to work on and the wildlife he used to see and he made a big fuss of Megan. He also told me some really grim stuff, like how he'd shoot a rabbit for supper and trap moles for their skins, and I told him I believe animals have as much right to life as we do, but I didn't get uptight with him because he was a dear, really.

I told him where I was going but not about the harvest mouse; I just said I had to deliver something to Mr Wheeler.

'Oh, he's a strange one 'e is, us has a laugh about 'e,' he said. It was at that point that I began to think he might be someone interesting.

Bransworthy is just a village like so many others, but the countryside round there is lush, lots of woods and little fields, really pretty. The man on the bus gave me directions to the farm and it took me and Megan about ten minutes to walk there; she was excited to be somewhere different and kept racing off and back to me again, grinning and barking. The sun was really bright so everything was clearly defined; the dark red hawthorn berries in the hedges, the flock of gulls following a plough, and there was that feeling in the air that lets you know that autumn is here and everything is ripe and ready to be picked.

I reached the farm and liked it straight away; there were chickens running around everywhere and a sheepdog on the doorstep who wagged his tail and tried to sniff at the shoebox, then circled round Megan and made friends with her. Dave was having his lunch - that's his name, Dave - and he asked me in and made me a goat's cheese and rocket ciabatta. He was younger than I expected and quite laidback and he's got a lovely smile, kind of warm and apologetic at the same time.

Of course he was really amazed when I told him my story. We still don't really know how it came about, it was a chance in a million really, but it seems that my harvest mouse actually did make the trip from wheat field to flour bag unscathed.

This is how we think it happened. He'd only been renting the farm for two years, having come down from London because he wanted a more natural lifestyle, and he'd done brilliantly. It's more of a smallholding than a farm because most of the land had been sold off, but it's plenty for one person, or two. The hens were a success and he could have sold the free range eggs three times over because people are realising now that all this factory farming stuff is well dodgy. He had a few Jacob sheep, just for the wool of course, and a goat for milk and lots of veggies and they all did great but there was still some more land, so he decided to try some wheat. It was a good summer and it grew quite well, but he found it was going to cost a fortune to have one small field harvested, so he taught himself to use a sickle. There were loads of old tools still lying about the farm and Dave's great like that, if he really wants to do something then he just keeps trying until he's got it right. Then he threshed it by hand which was really hard work and then he ground the grain. He admits that he was getting a bit tired of the whole thing by then and probably didn't make a very good job of it, but he was still amazed that he could have missed a mouse. I mean, not even his tail was damaged. Well, he tipped it all into bags and he was a bit worried when he saw how much straw was still in with the flour, but he took it down to the wholefood shop and of course they didn't want to know. After that it was easy to see how it happened. He sold it all on for next to nothing to a man he met in the pub who claimed he would use it for animal feed and there we are, one harvest mouse in the room of yours truly.

We released the mouse in the field where the wheat was grown. When we put him on the ground he sat up on his hind legs with the end of his tail curled round a blade of grass, and looked all around with those eyes like tiny jet beads. He made a couple of false starts then scampered off into the grass and was gone. Dave said their life span is quite short and that he probably didn't have long to live, but it wouldn't surprise me if this one was different.

We did wonder for a while whether we could develop the idea and market it. We felt it could really catch on, I mean, people like to think their food is natural these days so why not? Harvest mouse in flour, bee in honeycomb, fish in mineral water. Perhaps even butterfly in pot pourri. Probably the world isn't quite ready for that and anyway we both think creatures should be free and live naturally. But we've found something that's better than all that. Baby in belly. It's going to be awesome.

Aunt Lily

As she pushed open the gate, Marilyn saw that the red rose was on the grave as usual, a single spot of colour in the corner of the pallid November churchyard. She kept it in sight, walking up the steep path to stand in front of her aunt and uncle's stone, and read the few stark words as she did every year. She wondered again whether it would have been better to describe Lily as a loving wife, and again she decided that as Lily had not appeared to have loving memories of her husband, it did not much matter.

She crouched at the foot of the grave and flattened the grass with her hand before carefully placing her pot of chrysanthemums. The gales had scattered the last of the hedgerow leaves over the churchyard but Aunt Lily's grave was tidy, no doubt cleared by yesterday's visitor. The rose would have been placed there for the anniversary of her aunt's death, and she knew who was responsible. She was careful to arrive a day late to avoid the embarrassment of meeting him.

She spoke softly.

'You've got your red rose again, Aunt Lily.'

She stood in front of the grave for a few minutes then she turned and walked quickly back to her car, glad to be returning to her own less complicated life.

The first few miles were along narrow lanes made slippery by a layer of damp leaves so she concentrated on her driving, allowing her thoughts to stray only to domestic matters. Robert was cooking tonight so she had to call at the supermarket in Newton Abbot on the way home. It was artichokes and sherry vinegar he wanted this time. When she had made a show of protesting, asking what was wrong with the already abundant contents of the larder, he had whirled her around the kitchen in a tango and told her she should know to expect the exotic after four years of living with him. She smiled to herself. It was true; life was never dull.

When she reached the main road, her thoughts drifted back to her aunt and uncle. Even now it was easy to picture them. Aunt Lily was elegant in an understated way, always well dressed in subtle and unusual colour combinations which set off her chignon of white hair. By contrast Uncle Harry was a large jovial figure, as untidy as she was trim. He had a liking for practical jokes which entranced Marilyn when she was a little girl but were rather irritating as she grew up; a thrown tomato stalk became a spider, a five pound note was found between the pages of a newspaper. He would pause with raised eyebrows, ready to break out with his characteristically loud guffaw, while Aunt Lily regarded him with a thoughtful smile, much as one would a member of another species. Although her large dark eyes were capable of flashes of warm sympathy, her look was more often inward. She seemed complacent in her self-sufficiency and did not appear to need social contact or to have any close friends. Marilyn's attempts in later years to talk to her about books, something they should have been able to share, were met with a few pertinent comments and a change of subject.

Marilyn had seen them rarely since she was a child but things changed when Uncle Harry died. She was living alone in Plymouth by then and felt obliged to see her aunt more frequently now that she too was on her own, and soon fell into a habit of visiting on the first Sunday afternoon of the month. In her memory those visits always seemed to take place on hazy and overcast November days with the prospect of a lonely Christmas ahead. She would drive along the A38 and glance up at the muted colours of the distant wooded hills and the brilliance of the trees in the foreground, yellow sycamore, golden oak and brassy beech leaves, bursts of colour like the final flare of a firework before it falls and dies. The turning to the village was obscure and the lane that led to the house even more so; a deep, narrow way that was unsigned and wound down into a small, hidden valley. Aunt Lily's home for the last thirty years had been one wing of a large detached house which was approached by a tree-lined drive, and her entrance, being tucked away at the back, was never found by unwanted callers. If the weather was dry she would usually be in her secluded high-walled garden, pruning the climbing rose, raking leaves or on her knees trimming the edges of the lawn. She greeted Marilyn without any great enthusiasm and after a moment's awkwardness while she adjusted to having company, showed her some feature in the garden, a new shrub or some autumn crocuses pushing through. Marilyn remembered being shown the tiny oak saplings which had taken root where the grass grew long beneath the old tree and Aunt Lily potting one up for her.

'I doubt it will survive,' she had said. She never seemed to think Marilyn very capable.

Marilyn would offer to help and was usually given some little job to do where she could not cause too much damage, perhaps cutting back the nettles in the corner of the garden that had been allowed to grow wild since Uncle Harry died. It seemed that there was far too much work for Lily but she neither complained nor showed much interest in the results of her labours; indeed, although she seemed contented in her immaculate house and her garden, Marilyn had never known her to be passionate about anything.

If there was no gardening to be done Marilyn cleaned the windows or did chores which were too heavy for an elderly lady. Then her aunt made tea and they would sit in her tidy, pink and cream living room, she sitting majestically in the chair next to the fireplace and Marilyn trying hard not to sprawl on the sofa. They listened to the steady ticking of the glass-domed clock and Marilyn attempted to have a conversation. She would ask about her aunt's weekly visit to Exeter, for she had always spent one day a week shopping and having lunch in a favourite restaurant in the city, and enquire whether she did not find it tiring now. She did not, she said, for she always sat a long time over lunch. Marilyn talked about the past in the belief that this what all elderly people enjoyed, raking up memories about Uncle Harry's exploits when she was a child or about the old spaniel they used to have.

'Yes, I remember that,' she said with a polite smile.

She tried asking her about her courtship with Uncle Harry and she answered with the briefest of details. Marilyn had at first been hesitant about mentioning him for fear of upsetting her, but she seemed neither moved nor greatly interested. She grew quite concerned about her aunt, feeling she must be repressing her grief, and felt duty-bound to help her express her feelings.

'You must be very lonely at night,' Marilyn ventured.

'I have never minded being alone,' she answered in her measured way and again the conversation reached an impasse, to Marilyn's embarrassment and her aunt's apparent composure. On some occasions she would refer indirectly to Marilyn's divorce; it was apparent that she found this topic more interesting, but Marilyn was reluctant to describe the growth of indifference and minor infidelities that had led to the separation. Her aunt was also curious to know whether she managed to get out much in the evenings; she was seeing someone at that time but it wasn't going particularly well and her lack of enthusiasm must have been obvious.

'So you haven't found the right one yet?' Aunt Lily asked with that rare warm smile which transformed her. Marilyn mumbled something about not expecting to meet one person who would solve everything.

'You may, one day,' she replied and her complacent, faraway look returned.

Once, Marilyn called in, without warning, on her aunt's birthday to give her a bouquet of flowers, and was surprised to see a dozen roses arranged in a crystal vase on the hall table.

'Oh, you have some flowers already!'

'I always like to treat myself on my birthday,' her aunt replied as she ushered her into the living room. It crossed her mind that roses were an unusual choice and, as she faced the tedious drive home in the failing light, she told herself that her aunt was becoming far too solitary and that at least she had had some company for an afternoon, the only company she ever enjoyed now. It was always a relief to leave, but she felt a lingering regret that there was not greater warmth between them.

A short while after her last visit, the phone rang early in the morning. It was a nurse from the Royal Devon and Exeter Hospital telling her that her aunt had had a stroke, but was conscious and as well as could be expected. Marilyn left work early that day and went to see her. Aunt Lily had not aged very much over the years but now she seemed a very frail old lady, looking so small and alone in the hospital bed. Her mouth drooped at one side and a thin trail of saliva ran down to her chin; Marilyn longed to wipe it away but did not like to be so familiar as they had never even kissed. Her speech was rather slurred and she seemed anxious, her main concern being that she had missed going to Exeter that day, but she refused Marilyn's offer to buy anything she might need.

'Is there anyone I can phone for you?' Marilyn asked. Aunt Lily gave her a long, thoughtful look as if considering her properly for the first time, then turned wearily away and closed her eyes.

'No, there's no one you can phone.' It seemed that her neighbour had seen the ambulance and had contacted the few people who needed to know. 'Friends of your uncle's,' was how she put it. Marilyn arranged to pick up some nightdresses and toiletries on her way to the hospital the next day and, when she left, Aunt Lily thanked her for coming. For the first time she sounded as though she meant it.

Marilyn was again woken by the telephone the next morning and was told that her aunt had suffered another stroke during the night and had passed peacefully away. She took a day off work to make arrangements and another day for the funeral itself. Although she could not truly describe herself as bereaved, she did feel a sadness that a chapter of her life was now over; Aunt Lily had been her last close relative. The funeral was a sad little affair with just a handful of people, none of whom Marilyn recognised. Some distant cousins sent a wreath. She drove home immediately afterwards and spent a dispiriting evening alone.

When the will was read, Marilyn was surprised to discover that everything had been left to her. She spent the next two weekends at Aunt Lily's house sorting out her possessions and putting some aside to furnish the cottage she planned to buy when she had sold her own flat. It was a mundane task, for there was very little that was personal and she found it depressing that anyone could leave so little of themselves behind after nearly eighty years. There was the eclectic collection of books, the wardrobe full of clothes and a sad little assemblage of tins and packets in the larder which reduced her to tears when she found them. All Uncle Harry's things seemed to have been disposed of already and there was no sign that he had ever lived there, except for some photo albums in the loft. She wanted a few pieces of furniture and some books, and intended to keep the antique glass-domed clock, until she remembered its steady tick measuring out the hours, the days and the years, and put it aside to be sold.

There was one locked drawer in the dressing table which frustrated her until, on the last day, she found a little key in a vase on the window sill. When she opened the drawer she found a large ornamental box containing three piles of letters neatly tied with red ribbon and addressed to her aunt c/o Exeter Post Office. The box also contained a diamond and sapphire ring in a tiny velvet pouch, an empty bottle of very expensive French perfume, a diminutive Oxford English dictionary bound in leather, and two miniature Japanese carvings; a frog sitting on a lily pad and a nakedly entwined couple.

She quickly closed the drawer again and took a step back from the dressing table. The house felt very still; she went downstairs and walked through the bare living room and into the hall where boxes were stacked against the wall, but Aunt Lily was not there and perhaps never had been there in spirit. She returned upstairs and looked down from the bedroom window to the garden, where the weeds were already pushing through and the lawn edges needed cutting, then opened the drawer again and untied the bundles of letters. All the envelopes were addressed in the same handwriting and were carefully arranged by date; the very first some thirty years before and the most recent, addressed to this very house, just six weeks previously.

She spoke aloud; 'Forgive me, Aunt Lily,' then she took the first letter from its envelope.

She did not read them all nor did she read them thoroughly, quickly turning the page when the writer became intimate, skipping through the references to previous conversations and books and lovemaking. It did not take her long to realise that the letters were only written when meetings were impossible, and she remembered her aunt's weekly visits to Exeter.

She made herself a cup of tea and went into the garden to drink it. All the mourners at the funeral had been elderly, half a dozen couples and a few single women, but there had been one man on his own; he had been tall and distinguished-looking and had stood apart from the rest. She wondered whether to contact him – she had his address – but doing so would reveal that she had read the letters and would disrupt thirty years of privacy and, she suspected, his even longer marriage.

There was a cold wind; she fastened her coat and sat back on the garden seat. Years ago Uncle Harry used to sit here when they had tea in the garden and Aunt Lily sat on a reclining chair alongside the oak tree. He tried to play tricks on Marilyn and Lily, claiming some preposterous animal was behind them so that he could hide the plate of cakes when they turned. Aunt Lily never fell for it and refused to join in the fun, and only now did Marilyn recognise the hint of desperation in his efforts to amuse and the sadness that lurked in his eyes behind the hopeful smile.

She lit a bonfire in the garden that evening and watched the smoke being whipped away into the darkness by the gusty November breeze. As she stared up into the night she imagined she could see her aunt's face and it looked down at her with pity for having failed to find such happiness. It was then that she resolved that her life would change.

'And that was five years ago,' Marilyn announced to the empty car, as she drove into Newton Abbot after visiting the churchyard.

'What do you think, Aunt Lily, have I found the right one now?'

If she could see Marilyn now, would she draw parallels with her own life and perhaps reflect that she could have managed things differently? Marilyn was not inclined to judge her too harshly; divorce had not been an acceptable option for her generation, but the memory of Uncle Harry haunted her nevertheless.

She found the sherry vinegar and artichokes for Robert and picked up a bottle of wine and the peaches he liked. The supermarket was already decorated for Christmas, reminding her that she would soon need to start making plans, because this year she wanted to reciprocate the welcome that Robert's relatives had extended to her. She intended to invite them all over for Boxing Day; the house was big enough.

She had not bought a cottage as she had planned. She had pictured a narrow winding lane leading to a secret valley and a thatched cottage with thick cob walls and small-paned windows to give privacy and seclusion, but after Aunt Lily's death the thought of such a place made her feel uncomfortable. She waited, and she decorated her flat to make it a more attractive proposition when she was ready to sell. After a year of Robert's persuasive courtship and the tiresome travelling between their distant homes, she relented and, after a few months of discussion and searching, they bought a house together.

She put the shopping in the back of the car. After driving for twenty minutes she could see their home above the straight open road. On the southern edge of Dartmoor, high up on the side of a hill with a wide view over moorland and distant farmland, it was exposed to the full force of angry gales, to the warmth of the sun, and to the gaze of passers-by who could see right into the rooms if they cared to look.

She parked the car in the drive and ran up the steps to the front door.

'I'm back! Hello!'

'Just in time! Did you get the shopping? I was about to give up hope and make you beans on toast.'

He put his arms around her and they kissed.

'A likely story. Sorry, that journey always takes longer than I expect.'

She relaxed against him, suddenly tired.

He looked at her. He knew she was always apprehensive about visiting her aunt's grave.

'So, was there a rose this time?'

'Yes. Yes, there was. So he's still alive, out there somewhere.'

'Poor chap.'

He held her, and together they looked out of the window at the autumnal landscape; as they looked, the wind tore the last leaf from Aunt Lily's oak sapling which grew strong and true near the gate, whirling it up into the sky and away, until it was lost from sight.

The Best Christmas Present

Dennis was hoping to find a special present for his great-nephew; Christmas was for children really and Adam was the only child in his family. He reversed into a space in the Bridge Street car park and checked that each door of his old but cherished Ford Anglia was locked. He adjusted his scarf and fastened the top button of his overcoat because it had got a lot colder since the rain had cleared away, but it was good to be out, nevertheless. He glanced down the hill towards the river; although it was partially obscured by the Victorian stone-built town hall, it was still possible to see the long bridge and a narrow stretch of silvery water.

He didn't often come into the centre of Bideford these days. When his mother died and he no longer had to buy the meat and bread and vegetables from certain people, he started to shop at the supermarket once a week and continued even when he retired. But it pleased him to be in the town today because every street held memories for him, unlike the aisles of the supermarket.

He didn't have many presents to buy. He always bought his sister Nancy a box of chocolates and she had suggested a new torch for her husband Bill to light his way to bell-ringing practice. Their daughter Michelle could have chocolates too and there was no need to buy anything for her husband because he had skedaddled and had been seen around town with a girl barely out of her teens. That just left Adam. He wanted to get something really special for Adam.

It was only after lunch that he had decided to go out. It had been yet another wet and blustery morning and while eating his sandwich, he glanced anxiously out at his windswept garden and the broccoli plants that he should have staked more firmly. The television news was about war again and showed rubble-strewn streets, wrecked vehicles and groups of men in turbans who stood in the back of moving pick-ups, shouting and brandishing guns, then pictures of hungry women and children living in camps. Everything seemed to be going wrong in the world, even the weather. When he was a boy they never had summers of interminable rain or autumn winds that blew day and night for weeks, so perhaps those who talked about global warming were right after all. Staying indoors all the time, watching the news and thinking about all the changes in the world, could play on your mind especially when you lived alone. That was the mistake his friend Keith had made and he'd never been the same since, so Dennis made sure he got out for a walk every day whatever the weather, and he had the Classic Car Club meetings and the Model Railway Club to go to. You had to keep busy.

On Sundays there was lunch with Nancy and Bill; Michelle and Adam usually came too. He was a lovely lad, Adam. He would come running in, shouting,

'Uncle Dennis, Uncle Dennis!' his freckled face animated by a broad smile and his brown eyes alive with possibilities, and he would bounce all around Dennis with excitement at the game or trick or joke he had to tell.

'Slow down, boy, slow down, there's no need to make a song and dance of it,' Dennis would say.

Dennis reached the High Street and looked up at the decorations suspended across the street and the glittering trees erected over doorways, the illuminations drawing his gaze away from the gloomy sky beyond. The town was busier than he'd seen it for a while, and the bustle, the cold and the sparkling lights re-ignited a little of the seasonal excitement he used to feel when he was young.

The shops in Mill Street had their doors closed against the cold, but little bursts of warm air and snatches of Christmas music wafted out as customers entered. He looked shyly away from the Big Issue seller smiling at him from outside the Co-op and dived into the sweet shop that had been there for as long as he could remember. He chose two boxes of chocolates and was secretly pleased when the assistant remembered him from previous visits and wished him a Merry Christmas. As he walked along the old, narrow street to the hardware shop to buy the torch, he looked in the windows, hoping to see something that would suit Adam. The old toy shop had long since gone and in any case he didn't seem to be much of a boy for toys, although he was still only eight; he liked fast, bewildering computer games and he liked to be out and about, exploring new places and finding out about things, riding his bike. It was years since Dennis had been on a bike but he had wondered whether he should get one, especially now that Adam's dad wasn't around to take him out. Adam was considered old enough to go out for the day with his uncle now, so in September they had gone to a steam rally together. The exhibits were wondrous when seen through a young boy's eyes, and even eating fish and chips in the car while they sheltered from the rain had been fun, but there wasn't always something special like that to go to.

Mill Street was bustling with cheerful people carrying long rolls of wrapping paper under their arms and calling out greetings to each other, and Dennis saw several people to whom he could wish a Happy Christmas. Since he was last here, several of the old properties had been taken over by new businesses. It used to be all butchers, greengrocers and bakers when he was young, but now it was mostly cafes and places selling candles and ornaments for the home. He peered into one of the windows. There was a fat felt robin holding holly in its beak for £19, coloured wooden hearts to hang on the Christmas tree and piles of pink velvet cushions costing £30 each. It was a wonder how the owners were able to make a living because none of it seemed to be things that people needed. And there was nothing to suit Adam.

Michelle worried about the boy, especially since his dad had left. She had to increase her hours to make ends meet and Adam had to go home from school on his own. He wasn't doing too well at school, she said, which Dennis found extraordinary because he seemed as bright as a button and clever at so many things, but there was talk of him being rough and hurting children in his class and Michelle having to see the head teacher.

One recent Sunday when Michelle had to go to the supermarket after lunch, Dennis offered to take Adam out for a walk. They walked out along the Tarka Trail together and leaned on the parapet of the Iron Bridge watching the river flowing out towards the sea, carrying with it branches and leaves thrown down by the latest storm. Dennis asked him about school and Adam looked down and kicked the base of the wall. School was stupid, he said, and he named some boys he said he hated.

'I'm going to beat them up on Monday.'

Dennis wasn't sure what to say.

'You'll worry your mum if you don't behave yourself. You must look after her now that she's on her own.'

It didn't seem enough to say but not having had children himself he couldn't be sure what was right, so he changed the subject and instead pointed out a pure white egret flying upstream and circling slowly down to land with its wings raised like an angel. Adam stood still in wonder and the difficulty passed; he seemed happy again, holding Dennis's hand and skipping along in time to Dennis's steady walk and asking him, what does the egret eat? How does it catch the fish and does it eat other birds? Why not? Where does it go when the weather is cold and why does the tide come in and out?

'You'll wear me out, you will,' Dennis said. Adam would be all right after this little problem was over; he was such an intelligent, lively lad. Dennis had thought of offering to have him sometimes after school but how would he keep him amused? He had no computer and the homework would be quite beyond him. But it would be wonderful to know that the silence would be broken by that eager voice at the end of the day.

Dennis bought the torch and looked around at the displays. There were tool kits that might be suitable for a boy but he wasn't sure that Adam would be interested. He liked playing with Dennis's model railway but he wasn't mechanically minded. He wished he had asked Michelle if she had any ideas.

He went to the end of the street and decided to take a walk down to the Quay. He wasn't used to shopping and it would be a relief to see open skies and the wide view over the river.

Along the Quay, sparkling trees and white Christmas lights were beginning to glow as the afternoon grew dim; a fine mist drifted low over the Torridge and feathery clouds were tinged with pink from the setting sun. As a lad he used to go crabbing here. He used to ask the fishmonger in Mill Street for pieces of rotten fish – you'd never forget the smell – and attach them to his line and lower them carefully into the water. After a few minutes there would be several crabs attacking the fish with their giant pincers and he would haul them out and imprison them, sidling and scratching, in a bucket but he always threw them back in the end. On returning home, he would be sent straight out to the yard to wash. His father used to fish from the bridge alongside other men but that was a serious business designed to put food on plates and, although Dennis picked up a lot of fishing lore through listening to his father, he was never encouraged to join in.

A flock of silent starlings preparing to roost under the arches of the old bridge wheeled and turned above the river in the pale winter light, looking as small as insects as they rose and fell in perfect harmony against the fading sky, and his spirit soared with them. He was so lucky to have a family to share the festivities with! His sister was always so patient and kind, Bill a good-humoured sort and Michelle so lively, chattering away at a bewildering speed, at least until her latest trouble.

He remembered the first Christmas after Michelle was born, all those years ago, and how he had been so entranced by the baby's energy and intense interest in everything that he could hardly take his eyes off her. At the time he still hoped that he might one day meet someone and marry and have a family of his own, although even then he couldn't imagine how this could be accomplished. He had always been shy around women, and he didn't tend to meet many at the Model Railway Club.

This Christmas Day he had been asked to arrive at eleven o'clock as usual but would pick up Michelle and Adam first as, this year, they would be coming for the whole day; he could already picture Adam looking for him from the window and hear the excitement in his voice when he ran out. If the weather was dry, perhaps he and Adam could go for a walk in the afternoon because it was a long time for a boy to be cooped up inside.

He still had to find that present.

He wandered up the High Street. Some teenagers dressed as elves and a youthful Santa Claus pranced around on the pavement, stopping passers-by to collect for charity. Dennis fumbled in his pockets, embarrassed by the smiling young girl whose elfin coat exposed an expanse of green-stockinged thigh, and he hurried on to the accompaniment of their shouted thanks.

He stopped outside a shop selling mobile phones. The dazzlingly bright window held tiny phones suspended like jewels and next to each was a small card bearing incomprehensible numbers and letters. Adam said that he wanted a mobile phone but probably Michelle would buy him one. He had told Dennis that he too should have one so that they could send each other messages, which sounded intriguing but he would not know where to start. Perhaps one day he would go into the shop and ask.

He went into the pound shop and edged past towering displays of tinsel and plastic Christmas trees until he found the children's toys; there were some footballs and he picked one up to examine it.

'Doing your Christmas shopping then? I bought one of those for my grandson, no point spending a lot when you know they'll lose it after a day or so.'

The woman, whom Dennis recognised from somewhere, was wearing an overall and was arranging pink teddy bears on a shelf. He laughed carefully.

'No, that's right. You're right.'

He replaced the football on the shelf and stared at it as if he was considering it. He knew it was not of good enough quality. When she turned away, he made for the door.

He wandered on up the steep street and turned towards the market. It was years since he had been up here and he had heard that the market was not what it used to be, but the ornate stone and brick building was as imposing as ever. Being Thursday, the market hall was closed but he found that the arcade in Butcher's Row was open so he walked through, looking at the window displays of paintings, pottery and amusing wood carvings. There was nothing for Adam. He was beginning to despair of finding the right present and seeing his nephew's face light up with pleasure on Christmas morning.

He strolled along the pavement below the market, reluctant to return to his car. He would have to ask Michelle for ideas. He hoped she wouldn't suggest a computer game. He wanted to get something exceptional, something that had a purpose. He came to the end of the pavement and glanced idly at a tiny shop which formed the corner of the huge Victorian building. It had escaped his notice when he passed it the first time because there was no garish sign board to declare its purpose, no gaudy lights to attract attention; the small windows were barred for security. He stepped closer and peered in.

It was a fishing shop. In the window were displayed a few carefully selected silver and black reels, complex shiny things quite unlike the one his father had used, and inside he could see fishing rods reaching to the ceiling, forks for bait-digging, landing and keep nets, and hooks of all sizes. It was a shop for people who knew what they wanted; a shop that provided the chance of catching the fish of a lifetime providing one had this reel or this line; a shop that promised the fulfilment of dreams. Dennis stared into the window and he could feel his heart thumping.

He opened the door and went inside. The room was very quiet and small. A man sat behind a tall counter. Dennis cleared his throat.

'Do you have a rod suitable for a young lad?'

By the time he left with a long, thin parcel in his arms, his mind was buzzing with ideas and advice. He and Adam would go on their first fishing trip when the weather was fine and the tide was high; he knew to dig for bait rather than buy it because boys love the mud and the thrill of discovery; he knew about locations they could try for bass and flounder and mullet and to keep a record of tides and weathers. Dennis had quickly overcome his shyness when he discovered that the shopkeeper was a local man with whom he shared many acquaintances. He had been assured that new gadgets were not essential to start with because fish behaved the way they always had done, so as well as the light rod for Adam, Dennis had bought a new line and hooks for his father's old rod which was still out in the shed. It would do for now because he would be concentrating on teaching Adam before he did much fishing himself. They would learn together by practising, side by side, and before long the spring would come and the evenings would draw out and leaf buds would open on riverside trees and birds would sing. It wouldn't even matter if it rained. A drop of rain wouldn't bother him and Adam.

He walked down Bridge Street and there before him was the River Torridge. He crossed the road and stood on the long bridge where his father used to fish and he thought of all the little rivulets running down from the high lands of Devon, rushing through well-worn streambeds along the edges of fields and the sides of deep lanes, down into narrow river valleys and under old stone bridges until they met with the one river, the Torridge, swelling and widening its course as it flowed past Sheepwash, Beaford, Torrington and Weare

Giffard and on into Bideford, to this place where he stood in the cold evening air on the bridge.

The church clock struck four, ringing out over the glistening river with its fringe of Christmas illuminations, and he thought of dear Adam trudging home from school in the winter twilight. Below the arches of the bridge the starlings chattered as they settled into their night-time roosts and when he looked up, he saw that the sky had cleared and a single early star shone out over the town, and he knew that frost would form on the land tonight; along the length of the river the hills would be hung with sparkling trees and the air would sing with cold.

It would be a good Christmas, he was sure of that, and he was sure that the fishing rod was the right thing for Adam, but it would not be the best present; the best present, for both of them, would be all the times they would spend together throughout the year to come.

THE TURNING OF THE TIDE

Liz Shakespeare

Devon, 1871
Young and vulnerable Selina Burman from Clovelly and her
two young children are confined in the harsh environment of
Bideford Workhouse. She can only observe them from a
distance and despairs of a better future. Her prospects
improve when she meets Dr Ackland, a popular G.P.
committed to social change. He employs her as a servant in
his own household, despite the doubts of his wife and the
Bideford community, for whom any connection with the
Workhouse is a source of fear and shame. Selina's work gives
satisfaction, but her search for love and security does not
conform to the expectations of a middle class Victorian
family and threatens to damage both her own future and Dr
Ackland's career.
Set in Bideford and Clovelly, this novel draws on newspaper
articles, letters and census returns, and powerfully brings to
life the factual origins of the story.

'An immensely engaging story that captures the reader from
the first page.' *Historical Novel Review*
'A clever combination of fact and fiction, this book both
illuminates and entertains – an extremely gripping read.'
Family History Monthly
'Liz Shakespeare understands the period perfectly well,
describing the deprivation of the Union Workhouse as though
she had suffered it herself.' *Devon Family Historian*

Available from www.lizshakespeare.co.uk

FEVER
A Story from a Devon Churchyard

Liz Shakespeare

How many of us have wandered through a country churchyard and been moved by the memorials to young children? In this book the author sets out to discover the truth behind a number of graves dating from just one year in a nineteenth century Devon village. Her compelling investigation reveals the harsh reality of life in a small village before the days of effective medical care. By skilfully weaving social history, research and imaginative reconstruction she builds a sympathetic portrait of a community in the midst of adversity. We hear of strange remedies, the attempts of the clergy to help the stricken village, and the desperate poverty and over-crowding in farm labourers' cottages – the same cottages which are considered desirable today. It is a story common to many rural communities; it is impossible to remain unmoved by the knowledge that this story is true.

'Fever is a good read, well-researched and dramatized with sensitivity.' *Western Morning News*
'A mixture of social history, research and imagination produces this sympathetic portrait of a community struggling to survive in harsh conditions... this book is a valuable reminder of how hard life used to be.' *Devon Life*
'This book gave me a great deal of pleasure to read. Liz Shakespeare has carried out her research very thoroughly.' *Devon Family Historian*

Available from www.lizshakespeare.co.uk

THE MEMORY BE GREEN
An Oral History of a Devon Village

Liz Shakespeare

Within living memory village life has changed beyond recognition. Yet the old ways have not disappeared completely for they survive in the memories of our older neighbours. In this book men and women born early in the twentieth century recall a vanished way of life: a time when large families kept a pig to supplement a simple diet; every drop of water was carried from the village pump; the whole village turned out to help with the hay harvest; when everyone knew, and was often related to, everyone else and life was as slow and steady as the horse which pulled the plough.

'The Memory Be Green is a delightful insight into village life which will ring true in villages countrywide.' *North Devon Gazette*
'People with modern `romantic' views of pre-war rural life should read this book to obtain an insight into the reality of the experience. Events of great importance to the life of the village are lovingly described - the killing of the family pig, the role of the cattle drovers and their "wonderfully well-trained dogs", the communal efforts to get the harvest in, the village school and fondly-remembered childhood mischief.' *Western Morning News*
`As generations die out and people's memories are lost to posterity, books like this with their invaluable eye-witness versions of village life in quieter and more sedate though more punishing times, form an important part of our literary heritage.' *North Devon Journal*

Available from www.lizshakespeare.co.uk